DEATH RODE A MINIBUS

RONALD S. SEALES

AuthorHouse™ LLC
1663 Liberty Drive
Bloomington, IN 47403
www.authorhouse.com
Phone: 1-800-839-8640

Published by AuthorHouse   04/15/2014

ISBN: 978-1-4969-0471-3 (sc)
ISBN: 978-1-4969-0494-2 (e)

Library of Congress Control Number: 2014906878

This book is dedicated to the memory of Gladstone and Stephanie Johnson, both of whom had not only the gift of love within them, but also the courage to manifest it to the very end.

R.S.S.

Knavery's plain face is never seen till us'd.

William Shakespeare, *Othello*

This is a work of fiction. Names, characters, places and incidents either are the product of my imagination or are used fictitiously. Any resemblance to actual persons, living or dead, events or locales, is entirely coincidental and unintended.

Ronald S. Seales

Martin Brogan thought of the woman he left lying in his bed. A woman with whom he was romantically involved after knowing her for such a short time. Was the entire process just an orgasmic fling? Would Nadira Gobin walk out on him like his wife Olive did? He wrestled with those thoughts. And deep inside, a harsh reality gripped him. He was falling in love with the widow of a man whose death he was investigating.

CHAPTER 1

The minibus hung a right off the East Bank Highway onto Houston Access Road. It scampered through Meadow Bank, Alexander Village and Albouystown by way of Hunter Street.

It was 3:00 a.m. The night was as dark as a jackdaw's breast. Cocooning Georgetown in an oppressive blanket of gloom.

Traffic was sparse. Crickets chirped. Bats flashed across the horizon with random movements in their hunt for mosquitoes. And fireflies flickered their intermittent lights, like marauding glow worms hunting for mates.

But the cool morning air was extraordinary. Permeating the atmosphere with its unforgettable perfume of daisies, lemongrass and frangipani flowers.

The vehicle turned right on Princess Street into Wortmanville. Before long it hung another right on Cemetery Road and a left on Sussex Street. As if forging a circuitous path to North East La Penitence. Then it made a left onto Mandela Avenue in close proximity to the Repentir Cemetery.

Le Repentir Cemetery was situated north of Vlissengen Road. Close to the Mandela landfill. The place was a voluminous, sprawling and almost unembellished tract of mingled woodland, dotted by white tombs and headstones, lavish crypts and solitary monuments. Stretching from St.

Stephens Street to Mandela Avenue. It was a landscape that begged attention. Low and high brush meandered in profusion. Black sage, baby jamoon, cherry tomatoes and diverse shrubbery ran amok. And indigenous species of antelope, guinea, and coastal Bermuda grass scampered about the ground with a fierce intensity.

There was no security. No constables on duty, no police cruisers on patrol. Incandescent dome lights hung on the sides of high wallaba poles. Distantly spread.

No gates nor fences. Denizens encroached on the land with reckless abandon.

The minibus rolled up a dirt road from Mandela Avenue into the cemetery. The road was forever deserted. Especially at that time of the morning. The vehicle kept a steady crawl. An opossum dodged its front tires with only seconds to spare as the minibus crept past black sage, monkey apple trees and other shrubs.

It came to a stop under a sandbox tree.

The driver, a well-built man with a fierce, fleshy face, slightly yellow teeth and high cheekbones experienced elation. Excitement cascaded through his brain. He felt he had made a big score. That was his second time visiting the cemetery at that time in a nine month span. He was about to collect his spoils. Spoils so big that his fingers almost trembled in triumph. Then he whispered to himself as his tobacco-stained lips moved almost soundlessly. Calm man! Show control! You've done that before. Then he shut off the headlights and killed the engine. His pistol, a .38 Smith and Wesson, was still warm. He grabbed it from the front passenger seat and stuffed it between his belt. He lunged his right shoulder on the door and burst it open. Quickly he stormed out of the vehicle. His eyes, with a crazed look, raked the darkness.

Not a damn living soul was there. He mused. Then he pulled a collapsible shovel and a flashlight from the floor of the driver's seat. He knew that he was not into dumping bodies. As an old country boy from Better Hope on the East Coast, he'd rather do things the old fashioned way. Bury the man. The soul would not go to hell. That was his belief.

The man walked down a steep incline about twenty-five feet from the minibus as the beam of the flashlight guided his steps. He stopped at a grassy patch. His eyes giving the landscape a long, searching look. Making sure he knew where he was. In the event of him having to run, he knew where to go. The graveyard looked no different at night as compared to day, he thought. Grave markers and tombs. Crypts and monuments, big or small. Well-kept or dilapidated. It made no darn difference. When you kick the bucket, you're history. Period.

There was no moon. No adverse weather condition. He pocketed his flashlight because starlight enabled him to see. His night vision was second to none, he reckoned. Quickly he cleared away a path between the coastal Bermuda grass and started to dig. Five minutes. Fifteen minutes went by. He had opened a hole about four-feet deep and five-feet long. The gray dirt got softer the further he went down. A walk in the park, he figured. Easy stuff. As a minibus driver, he stayed in shape by hauling luggage. And mindful of his diet. But he smoked like a sailor.

Then he stuck the shovel in the dirt and clambered toward the minibus. He opened the back passenger door. A man was lying on his back across the back seat. Dead as a doornail. Blood was splattered everywhere. A bullet hole was in the center of his chest and another to his right cheek. Exposing his teeth.

The driver tore off the dead man's jewelry. Rings, watch and chain. Then he rummaged through the pockets. Bingo! He found what he was looking for. Eight thousand dollars in United States currency. Plus the dead man's passport. United States of America. A look of rapture gripped his face as a tide of joy washed his brain. He fought for composure. Don't get carried away, something within him whispered. Get your shit together, asshole.

Then he whipped a pair of heavy work gloves from under the driver's seat. He donned them. He held the body by the ankles and dragged it down the incline. Blood left a trail along the coastal Bermuda and antelope grass. It didn't bother him any. The elements would take care of that, he pondered.

His breathing was labored when he got the body to its destination. The graveside.

"You're a heavy little bastard," he mumbled.

Then he let go of the corpse's ankles and emitted a heckling laughter in his throat.

Without any effort, his face lit up with malicious delight. He kicked the dead man into the grave and started to cover the body with dirt.

He looked at his watch. Four thirty in the morning. Far across the eastern horizon, dawn was breaking. Nightbirds darted across the sky.

"You son of a bitch," he muttered, talking to the dead man. "You ain't makin' it back to New York. Your folks be looking for you all over town. I ain't got no time to give you a better burial. I screwed around long enough. Almost done. Gotta get to hell outa this place."

Within ten minutes, he succeeded in completely covering the body. He leveled off the grave and scraped some grass over the freshly turned dirt. About finished, he reckoned. Just one more thing. The thing that would keep the Brickdam sleuths off his trail. Then he went by a small canal that ran through that part of the cemetery. He pulled off the gloves as he went on his knees. The water was black and laden with duckweeds and other aquatic plants. Green and yellow pond frogs croaked from their watery lairs. He washed his hands without soap as best he could. And quickly he washed the dirt off his shovel and headed up the incline. He opened the dead man's suitcase. And again he marveled at his fortune. Designer clothes, toiletries and miscellaneous items. A sudden stab of anxiety flashed across his guts. He stepped back. Again he chastised himself for losing his composure. Could not afford to have that happen. It diminished a man's thought process, he reasoned. And then it would be a difficult ordeal to pick up the pieces.

With an old T-shirt, he wiped away the blood and dried out the vehicle. He stood back and reckoned he had done an excellent job. Of sorts. Covering his dark twisted trail. Then he whipped out a cigarette from his pack and struck his lighter. Satisfaction caused his pupils to dilate. He was careful to dot his letters that needed dotting. And crossing his Ts. Then an elaborately casual feeling of achievement enveloped his mind.

About to wrap things up, he muttered. Just one other item. The bloody T-shirt. The object that would let the boys on Brickdam know what had happened. No. He wasn't that dumb. He had to get rid of that shirt.

Then he shrinked away in silence. Moving between tall trees, shrubbery and long-forgotten grave stones. Dodging around those objects. While thick elephant grass and fern lay underfoot. Branches of carrion crow bush, black sage and other low trees, slowed his momentum. Their leaves, like green, ghoulish tentacles, picked and plucked at his body.

Then he found the object of his search. A sandbox tree. Quickly he balled up the shirt, pushed it under some outcrop roots and covered it with dirt and fallen leaves.

He turned on his heels and headed back to the minibus. The quiet voice of the wind and the raspy sound of his breathing did not stop him from hearing the palpitating beats of his heart. One day he thought he had to quit smoking and see a good doctor.

He got into the minibus and fired the engine. He got back on the dirt road and made a left turn on Mandela Avenue. The vehicle was headed northeast towards the town of Felicity.

CHAPTER 2

It was 7:30 a.m. Friday during March 1998. Georgetown was coming alive after a long night of slumber. A melancholy sun, as if intoxicated by sleep, was attempting to show its face across a crimson, orange and blue horizon. A man called Mohan Basdeo sat behind the wheel of his minibus. The vehicle was headed east on the Liliendaal Expressway. Its destination was Felicity. A town sandwiched between Better Hope and Success off the Atlantic Coast. Basdeo reached for a pack of cigarettes from his glove compartment. He pulled one out, planted it between brown parched lips and ignited the tobacco. Prodigious eyes depicting ill omen were focused on the highway.

Traffic swelled by the minute.

Then, the events that transpired hours ago, gave his face a dubious expression.

It was a phone call he remembered. He was moving passengers from Werk-En-Rust to Prashad Nagar. No reason for anxiety, he figured. Just another passenger calling to be picked up.

"Hello," he answered.

"Mohan!"

"Yes, this is Mohan."

"You know who this is?"

"Can't recall. Lots of people call me every day."

"This is Joseph, man. Joseph Pollard."

"Yes, I remember now. The boss man at the airport. We worked together a couple of months ago."

"Yes. That's right. You put away that man real good."

"So what's happening, Joe?"

"You got any time after midnight tonight?"

"Sure. You know bus drivers like me gotta hustle. Not like you making money sitting down."

"This one is like taking candy from a baby."

"Like nine months ago?"

"Yes. A plane load of New York Guyanese is coming home to visit. The BWIA flight lands after midnight at Cheddi Jagan International Airport."

"How do you know some passengers are loaded?"

"Mohan, you know better than to ask me such a question. I'm in charge of Customs and Immigration on the midnight shift. When I say something, I mean it. One or two passengers got money."

"Well, you're the man in charge on the graveyard shift. Who am I to question you?"

"You're damn right. When I say so, it's so. That crap is written in stone."

"So when do I get there?"

"Be at the airport about 11:30 p.m. Stay in the parking lot with all the other vehicles until I call you, right."

"OK, boss man."

Mohan Basdeo pocketed his cell phone. A spasm of skepticism crossed his face. He wanted to avoid any traps or pitfalls. Dumb trust, he thought, made him swallow hook, line and sinker. And five years in a United States penitentiary.

That was twelve years ago in 1986. He was forty years old and married to a U.S. citizen. He lived in Queens, New York. And worked for Fed Ex, the second largest shipper of packages in the United States.

Things were going fine. He made every day deliveries to the boroughs of the Bronx, Manhattan and Staten Island as a truck driver.

The money was good after five years on the job. One summer he left his wife in New York and came back to Better Hope in Guyana to visit his ailing father. Unfortunately his father passed. Colon cancer took him out. Just as it did his mother.

He buried the old man and two weeks later, he journeyed to Cheddi Jagan International Airport for a flight back to New York City. Serendipitously, he crossed paths with a well dressed and eloquent speaking man on his way to the terminal.

"I see you're on your way to the Big Apple, Mister."

"Sure am. Just buried my old man."

"Sorry about your loss. Wonderin' if you can do a man a favor."

"What's that? Man, I don't even know you."

"Dropping a suitcase to a friend in New York."

"He'll be at the airport?"

"Yes. He'll be there."

"Any dope in that suitcase?"

The bony shouldered man with a flaring nose and flabby arms studied Mohan before answering.

"Yes. I got to be honest with you."

"Man, if that's the case, it will cost you some money for taking that suitcase all the way to New York."

"How much you want?"

"First, lemme know what kinda' dope you got there."

"Cocaine."

"What's the value on the streets?"

"Two hundred and fifty thousand. That's U.S. currency now."

"I'll take fifty grand up front to transport that dope. That's U.S. money."

"You got it. Let's go to the men's room. I'll pay you the money."

"OK."

Mohan followed the man to the bathroom. The man gave him five wads of U.S. currency totaling fifty thousand dollars.

"That's it, man. A light-skinned fellow with a red shirt and blue jeans will be waiting for you at Air Lingus Terminal B."

"You got it, man. What's your name?"

"Walter Jarvis. Call me Walt. What's yours, man?"

"Mohan Basdeo."

"Are you a Georgetown man?"

"No. East Coast."

"That's close enough man, I'm GT. You have a safe trip to the Big City."

"OK, Walter, later."

They parted ways. Mohan Basdeo grabbed his suitcase and the one he was transporting and went through customs.

A vivacious expression blanketed his face as he took his seat on the plane. Fifty thousand dollars. Just like that. His eyes blinked with incredulity as his doughy face stared straight ahead with a haughty disbelief.

Five hours later the plane touched down at Kennedy Airport in New York City.

Unknown to Basdeo, Guyana Police were investigating Walter Jarvis for narcotics smuggling. And he, Basdeo, had become the fall guy in a sting operation. A call was made to the Port Authority Police in New York City. A passenger named Mohan Basdeo was the owner of a suitcase containing cocaine. The contraband was being transported from Georgetown to New York for sale on the streets.

Orders were given to allow Basdeo to claim the brown suitcase from the baggage carousel. Then an arrest was going to be made.

Meanwhile Walter Jarvis was in police custody in Georgetown. Unknown to Jarvis, someone had tipped off airport police. They had him under surveillance even as he spoke to Mohan Basdeo. He was nabbed by lawmen as soon as the plane left the airport for New York City.

Hours later Basdeo was arrested in New York. Charges of smuggling narcotics and violation of customs regulations were made against him. The Federal Bureau of Investigation was called in. The case was prosecuted by the U.S. Attorney in the Department of Justice. Mohan Basdeo was sentenced to five years in a federal penitentiary in the state of Kansas. He was released at age forty-five. His green card was revoked and he was deported to Guyana. Basdeo never saw his wife again.

But years after in Guyana, he continued to dip and dabble into illegal activity. The benefits were good. Nine months ago his buddy, Joseph Pollard, let him in on a deal at the airport. Pollard used him for his gun and his brutality. Basdeo took his victim out and walked away with tons of money. That was after Pollard and him split their spoils.

It was just hours ago. He sent a man to his maker for the second time in as many months. And there he was on the expressway to Felicity. Just eager to share his booty with his cohort, Joseph Pollard. At fifty-two, he thought with his weathered complexion and aging body, that his actions were far from unjustifiable. He was honestly attempting to make a living smuggling drugs, when the trap came down on him.

That bastard, Walter Jarvis, he thought. The man set him up. And his freedom was wrenched from him. New York City police said the dope was valued at two and a half million dollars on the streets. That was when he realized that Jarvis, that piece of garbage, had lied to him. The man pulled wool over his eyes. He was his sucker.

Animosity for Walter Jarvis, his nemesis, caused his brows to furrow deeply. He pledged that one of those days he intended to plug him up his rectum. Because the consequences of the man's hustle would stay with him for years to come. Especially the loss of his green card and his wife. She ended contact with him two months after he was imprisoned. Without telling him anything.

But he sensed the subtle signs of her deceit. They were predictable. Her phone was disconnected. His letters to her in Queens, New York, were returned to him in prison.

How callous could a woman get, he grumbled, as his eyes narrowed with contempt. All those years, he worked his ass off at the Federal Express. Only to be reduced to that measure. A lowly inmate in a federal pen.

Then he came to the realization that there was no reciprocity in his relationship with his wife from the beginning. He fattened the woman like an overfed frog in a meadow. Just for other snakes to swallow. And the chips fell where they had to.

But by some means he trusted Joseph Pollard, even though deep within his brain there was some feeling of malice for the airport supervisor. Pollard was Afro-Guyanese and in Basdeo's culture, it was taboo for him to be taking orders from Pollard.

Then he remembered the time they crossed paths. It was somewhere between Better Hope and Felicity on the East Coast of Demerara. Pollard's car sustained a flat tire on the highway. That same evening Basdeo was on his way home from Success after dropping off some passengers. Having seen a well-dressed burly man on the highway by a disabled car, Mohan Basdeo offered his help. He assisted Joseph Pollard to replace the damaged tire. And the rest between the men was history. They became buddies and drank beer together in Better Hope and Felicity. Basdeo told Pollard about his times and travels in America.

"Are you serious, Mohan? You actually lived in America," Pollard asked one day in surprise.

"I shit you not, Joe. I lived in New York City for years, man."

"What in hell are you doing back in Guyana?"

"I screwed up, Joe. I lost my wife, my job, and every friggin' thing behind some crap."

"What's that?"

"I tried to smuggle some dope through JFK Airport and got caught."

"So they tossed your ass back here."

"Yes. That's right."

"Don't worry. We can make some money."

"What you're talkin' about Joe?"

"In my job as supervisor, I know who are the passengers coming to Georgetown with money."

"So."

"I'll funnel you the information. You pick up the airline passenger in your minibus after he exits the terminal. And along the way to Georgetown, you'll do the rest."

"Sounds good, Joe."

"It's a damn money maker. We'll split everything down the middle."

But Basdeo's venomous feelings for Joseph Pollard were mild as compared to that which he harbored for airport security. Men sniffing around. Watching people from behind walls and hidden partitions with one way mirrors. At both Cheddi Jagan International and JFK airports. Looking into bags of passengers and their suitcases as if trying their hardest to get people into trouble.

It caused him five long years of his life in the slammers and a wife who didn't look back. She didn't give a monkey's butt if he was alive or dead. As a result, being tossed back to Guyana only burgeoned his resentment for everyone. Strangers coming to Georgetown with fancy clothes and sweet smelling perfumes and colognes, talking trash about how good it was to be in America. His disdain and resentment only intensified. There was a legitimate reason in his action, he thought. He felt compelled to continue his mad chronology of human carnage. Despite the risks. Then he thought of his youth. Growing up in Better Hope. He wanted to be a soldier in the Guyana Defense Force. Real bad. In addition to the potential risk and the possibility of being killed by a Venezuelan sharp shooter, he wanted to carry a gun. And wear a green uniform. Women would admire him. He liked everything about the idea of being a soldier. But his mother was against the whole idea. And in retaliation, he burned the neighbor's farmhouse to the ground. He was only eighteen and his father knew that he was responsible for such an act. But never confronted him. He remembered looking into his father's eyes at dusk that day. He envisioned wells of rage and disappointment. The older man looked away and spat on the ground.

CHAPTER 3

It was 12:00 noon that same Friday in March. A woman made a call to police headquarters on Brickdam. Her voice was high and hysterical.

"Calm down, madam, "the dispatcher was saying. "What's your name and address? Tell me your problem. We'll send an officer over."

Within ten minutes, a police cruiser pulled up at 135 Burchell Street in Subryanville. An Indo-Guyanese woman about fifty with a cinnamon complexion and long, charcoal-colored hair stood on the sidewalk. Her dark, deep-set eyes appeared haunted by an inner turbulence.

The cop got out of his car. His face was fierce and repulsive.

"Are you Nadira Gobin?"

"Yes, Officer. I'm Nadira Gobin."

"What's the problem?"

"It's my husband."

"What's going on with him, ma'am?"

"He flew in this morning at 1:00 a.m. from New York. He hasn't called or made any contact with me. He was to meet me here."

"Did you call the airline?"

"Yes. BWIA landed at 12 midnight. They said he cleared customs."

"Do you think he may have gone to a girlfriend's house?"

"No, Officer," the woman answered as her face was etched in desperation. "We've been married for twenty-five years. My husband was faithful from day one. He never cheated on me."

The policeman pulled a notepad from his shirt pocket and took the woman's name.

"Is this your address?"

"No, Officer. We live in Brooklyn, New York. We're here in Georgetown visiting family. My sister lives here."

"What's your address in Brooklyn?"

"That 637 DeKalb Avenue."

"You guys don't have any ongoing problems do you? You and your husband."

"No, Officer. I flew in two days ago. My husband stayed to take care of some business in Manhattan and follow after. I don't know of any trouble."

"What's your husband's name?"

"Cyril Gobin."

"Ma'am, it has been twelve hours since your husband disappeared as you're alleging. After twenty-four hours if he doesn't get in contact with you, we'll file a missing person's report."

"That's all, officer?"

"Yes. We will not go looking for him at this point. It's too early. Besides no one knows what may have happened for sure."

"OK, Officer."

"Call us if he doesn't come home by midnight."

"Sure, Officer. Thank you."

Nadira Gobin, a lean woman with beady ebony eyes and a gracious, feline face turned from the street and crossed the sidewalk. If it was another woman she reasoned, where did she go wrong? Why would Cyril want to do such a thing? Twenty-five years ago, he showed up with her father at their home in Big Diamond. Her life shifted. It didn't take long to find out that their marriage produced a son. But trouble came to the family in New York when that son decided to choose a black American woman as his wife. The family was devastated. But her offspring stuck to his resolve. He admonished his parents with a voice livid with exasperation. Religion or not, he thundered, he had the right to choose whomever he wanted to be his wife.

Nadira agreed. She found a point of balance in the relationship between herself and her son's wife. But her husband Cyril spoke of his daughter-in-law with irrational detachment. For years he estranged himself from his son and refused to visit his two grandchildren. Ten years ago, they crossed paths at Cyril's mother's funeral in Brooklyn. Cyril maintained that he was a Hindu. And it was wrong for his son to marry a black Christian woman outside of his religion.

That day in Subryanville, she thought of her son and his wife of African pedigree. Two people with similar mind sets. They nurtured resolve. Both had college education and good jobs. And probably both had tons of people who were disappointed in them. That's tough shit, she mused.

But it was time her husband came to grips with reality. They were living in the USA. Not Guyana. Where culture and tradition is paramount. Even to the point of pain, suffering and death.

The woman ascended the stairs. That day Georgetown was hot and sultry. And again the possibility of another woman invading her space caused her eyes to be filled with a troubled look. How could a woman be so unscrupulous and vicious? The question cascaded through her mind. For someone to steal her man was the last thing she had ever contemplated. The interloper, if one existed, was like the harpy eagle, she figured. A Jezebel and a bitch. She might have seduced her husband and was at the point of breaking up her marriage. She wanted to just lay her hands on that mysterious creature. That living entity who might have arrived in Guyana like a wrecking ball. Ready to devastate her life. That other woman was somewhere with Cyril, she reasoned. What a whore!

Two hours later Nadira Gobin got in a car with her sister and brother-in-law. They headed south on the East Bank Highway. The man pulled on a cigarette as ambivalence clouded his mind.

"Where could he have gone?" he was able to ask.

"The bar probably," his wife answered. "There are a few of them around the airport."

"Sometime ago he went off on a binge in Queens, New York. But he went to AA and took care of his problem," Nadira Gobin said. "Besides no one in his right mind will fly in from New York, stay at a bar for more than twelve hours and not get into contact with his family."

"Guess you're right," the man answered.

Forty-five minutes later the vehicle sped through Big Diamond, Nadira's old hometown. On rainy days, the streets were turned into canals. Snakes and other reptiles were everywhere and houses sagged along the highway.

Within an hour they were in the parking lot of Cheddi Jagan International Airport. It was about 3:00 p.m. that early evening in March. The sun played hide and seek with some dark, heavy clouds. A look of a hard, wet rain lingered across the sandhills of Tacama, far to the east.

The three people walked towards an outpost. It housed a security guard. He watched people as they entered the main area of the terminal.

"May I be of assistance?" he asked.

"We're looking for a man about fifty-five years old. Five-feet-ten inches and weighing about two hundred pounds," Nadira responded. "He's East Indian."

"Was he flying in or out of Georgetown?"

"He came in at 1:00 a.m. this morning on BWIA from New York," Nadira answered.

"Ma'am, the person you're looking for could have gone anywhere. We never keep tabs on passengers once they leave the terminal."

"My husband called me at 5:00 p.m. yesterday. He told me he was boarding a plane. BWIA flight number 283 from JFK. He said he was going to be here at midnight."

"Did your husband ever land in Guyana?"

"Sure. The airline said he cleared customs."

"So you're sure he landed."

"That's right," Nadira said.

"Ma'am, is everything OK with your husband? Is he sick, confused or has a physical problem?"

"My husband doesn't have any problems. He's in his right mind."

"Lady, I wish I can give you the answer you're looking for. Unfortunately, I can't. But if you care to drive around the airport and ask people living around the area, it may help some."

"Thank you."

Nadira, her sister and her brother-in-law drove around the airport. People erected small low houses on the hillsides and foothills. And in the valleys and close to the Madewini Creek. They planted their crops, raised their families and existed in an environment so harsh that it was almost forgotten by time. No one saw anyone fitting Cyril's description.

They were about to leave the perimeter of the airport when their attention was caught by a small, isolated frame dwelling. It lay flat on the white sandy ground. Tall paragrass and low bushes shrouded a shadowy front porch. A small brown mongrel for a dog barked at the car as it stopped in the front of the house. An eeriness enveloped the area. The front door was opened wide. On the front porch was a rocker. The eyes and ears of the three people took a moment to adjust as they got out of the car. A fierce and pungent smell of alcohol was heavy in the atmosphere. On the rocker lay the unmistakable shape of a human being sitting partly upright but slumped against his right arm. The person was covered from head to toe with a checkered bed sheet. A long line of bougainvilleas ran along a rail to the individual's left. The three edged their way towards the figure. Nadira felt a rush of heat to her face. Cyril might have drank himself to a stupor and was attempting to sleep it off before coming home. Anticipation caused her face to beam. Her brother-in-law was drooping to a crouch as he got closer to the character. He reached for a corner of the checkered sheet and yanked it off the form. It was an old Amer-Indian man. He appeared dead for more than forty-eight hours. Decomposition was taking shape. An empty one liter rum bottle sat on the porch besides the man's feet. Death hung everywhere. Like mist in a valley. Nadira's brother-in-law had no doubt that the man might have drank himself to death. He got out his cell phone and called Madewini Police.

The following day Nadira Gobin went to Police Headquarters in Brickdam and reported that her husband was missing more than twenty-four hours ago.

The sergeant at the front office filled out a form taking all necessary information.

"OK, ma'am," the gap-toothed man with an insect-like face concluded. "Sign on these dotted lines."

"What next Officer?"

"We'll put a detective on the case and you'll hear from us."

"Thank you."

CHAPTER 4

Two weeks went by. Nothing was heard.

"Come on and eat, Nadira. Dinner's ready," her sister Angela said. "I cooked eggplant curry and fish."

"All right," Nadira answered.

Nadira went in the kitchen, sat down and stared at her plate. She didn't want to eat. There was that abyss of melancholy that caused a stab of fear, deep in her belly. She was unable to shake her feelings.

"Eat something, Nadira. I know you're worried about your husband," Angela said.

"You're right. I'm thinking about Cyril. So bad that I don't feel like eating."

Then her breath became raw in her throat as she thought that something might have happened. It was a deceptive calm before a big storm, she figured. With heavy black clouds hanging along the horizon of her mind.

Nadira sat at the table. She picked at her food. And hoped that her negative thoughts of Cyril would disappear. But they smothered her. Yet she wanted to face up to the whole ordeal in a positive way. But still, thoughts that he might have run into some kind of misadventure kept filling up her head.

Then psychosomatic affects of her anxiety were taking shape. Her back became sore and stiff. Her head pounded. She shivered, hunched up her shoulders, and shut her eyes.

Then she rubbed them with the tips of her fingers until all she saw were spots and flashing lights. Her light blue nightwear, pants and top of satin, hung loosely about her frail body.

For some unknown reason, she was wearing Chanel No. 5. Just like in years gone by. That sophisticated fur-coat-and-diamond fragrance that started that Mother's Day at Macy's in Manhattan. That unforgettable moment that quickened her husband's pulse. For two decades, Nadira Gobin had awaited a visit to Georgetown with the breathless anticipation of a young woman at her first dance. She did not leave a stone unturned during her preparation to see Guyana after staying away so long.

That day in Subryanville, all she felt was dread. And a depression etched with sorrow and panic. What was a wife to do when her husband was nowhere to be found?

Then her cell phone rang!

Her fingers trembled as she pulled the phone towards her. She answered it. The caustic voice of a man caused her breath to quicken.

"Are you Mrs. Gobin?"

"Yes," she answered, her heart racing. "Who are you?"

"I'm Cyril's friend."

"Really. Where's Cyril?" she asked, her voice growing frenzied.

"I know where he is."

"Where is he?" her voice carrying an edge of anger mingled with contempt.

"I got him. He's safe with me."

"Why are you holding my husband? You have no right to do so. Who are you?"

"Who I am doesn't matter. He owes me money."

"That's not true. He doesn't owe you anything. I'll call the police!"

"Mrs. Gobin, go ahead and call the cops. You'll never see Cyril again. I swear."

"So, how much money my husband owes you and for what?"

"Never mind for what. Just pay me twenty thousand in U.S. currency and your man is free to come home to you."

"Let me speak to my husband."

"That's not going to be possible."

"Why?"

"That's not part of the deal."

"So what do I do now?"

"Simple. Just follow instructions. No cops. If you do notify the police, I'll kill your husband. That's no bullshit now."

"I'll do anything to save my husband's life."

"You drive to South Ruimveldt Gardens. Stop at the junction of Caneview Avenue and Greenheart Street. You'll see a black garbage pail at the corner. Put the money wrapped in a plastic bag in that pail."

"When?"

"Tonight. You bitch. Tonight!"

"Sir, I don't have that kinda money at home. You'll have to give me some time to go to the Bank of Guyana."

"How much time you want woman? Come on. Let's get this over with!"

"Tomorrow at 9:00 p.m. I'll put the money in the pail. Just as you said at the corner."

"You better do that. Or else your man will be comin' back no more!"

"Please, mister. Don't hurt my husband!"

The man ended the conversation without responding to her entreaty.

Nadira reeled with astonishment. Like a cold fist was squeezing down on her heart. Then her control exploded. Lurching forward, arms flailing. She screamed. A raw, unintelligible and incoherent cry.

"Angela, Kishore!" she screamed as she banged on her sister's bedroom door.

The couple spilled out into the living room with bated breath.

"What is wrong Nadira?" Angela asked as she winced in astonishment. Kishore, her husband, stood there in stunned silence.

"It's a man," Nadira said with a cracking voice. "He called me with Cyril's phone a few minutes ago. He said he knows where my husband is."

"What!" Kishore said, gnashing his teeth. "And why can't Cyril come home?"

"He wants me to give him money before he lets Cyril come home. He's holding my husband hostage."

"His ass is crazy!" Kishore snapped.

"How much money he wants?" Angela was able to ask.

"Twenty thousand dollars in U.S. money," Nadira answered, her muscles tensing.

"That man, whosoever he is, belongs in the madhouse in Berbice. People just don't pick up money from the street," Angela blurted in defiance.

Nadira sobbed as her face grew haggard with worry.

"What did you tell him Nadira?" Kishore asked with an irate expression.

"I told him I'll give him the money tomorrow at 9:00 p.m."

"What! Are you serious?"

"He told me to put the money in a garbage pail in South Ruimveldt Gardens at the corner of Caneview Avenue and Greenheart Street if I want to see my husband again."

"And where will Cyril be?" Kishore asked.

"He'll let him go from his car."

"I think he's lying," Angela joined in. "We should call the police and let them know about this."

"That's a good idea," Kishore said with a tight pinched face. "He called you with Cyril's phone. How did he get Cyril's phone? There's something going on. I don't like the smell of this. Angela is right. Let's go to the police and report this."

CHAPTER 5

The next evening, a somber new moon hung wantonly among low clouds as an unmarked police cruiser crawled lazily on Caneview Avenue. Its direction was due east.

It was 8:25 p.m. when the unmarked car made a stop. It nestled among other vehicles parked on the curbside. About half a mile from a garbage pail. Two cops sat in the back seat of the squad car. One male, the other female. The woman was dressed in street clothes like the other ranks. The front seat cop occupying the passenger seat raked the streets with a pair of binoculars. He was a mammoth of a man. An elephant-sized guy in a black T-shirt that hollered for compassion against his portly gut. He allowed the binocular to rest on his chest. When he spoke his voice was low and husky.

"There's no activity up there. No one on the streets."

"You're right. Looks awfully quiet," the cop in the driver's seat responded.

"I'll drop the parcel in the pail if you want me to, Sarge," the back seat cop suggested to the big man.

"No. We'll go as planned. If he's out there looking at the drop site and sees you, we'll blow our cover. He's out there. Somewhere. That I know for sure. May be working alone or with someone else. However this lowlife may be armed and dangerous. We don't want him to know that cops are here, waiting to snatch him up. The undercover police officer, acting as Mrs. Gobin, will drop the package where he instructed her to put it. Remember guys, her safety is our responsibility. We gotta watch her back like a hawk watching a chicken," the sergeant ended as he brought the binoculars to his eyes.

It was 8:45 p.m. The undercover woman, with a sari on her head and armed to the teeth, slipped out of the squad car. She carried a neatly packaged object wrapped in plastic in her hand. It was to be twenty thousand dollars in U.S. currency based on the agreement with the mysterious man. But it was far from that. In reality it was a bundle of old newspaper cut and stacked together like currency. The tormentor was in for a shock as big as South Ruimveldt itself, she reckoned.

Sweat ran down into her eyes. She used the back of her hand to wipe it away as she forged ahead with mincing steps. Her eyes darted maniacally, dissecting objects out of the gloom. A woman walking her dog. A grazing donkey and a solitary street sign. Everything that night caused her eyes to be haunted by some inner anxiety.

It was 9:00 p.m.

She made the drop and stood on the sidewalk, eyes flashing, teeth gnashing and stomach knotting. Adrenaline cascaded through her arteries as her veins throbbed at the temple. Her gun afforded her comfort.

She stood there for about eight minutes. A long, long time or what she perceived to be an eternity. Pesky night insects nor the cry of an eager puppy in the distance did not trespass on her thoughts. Only a dull, empty ache gnawed at her soul. Her disenchantment for the freeloader, whoever he was, welled up within her like magma in the belly of a volcano. She glanced in all directions with cold speculation. Then she came to the realization that the con artist did not show. She knew he was tucked away somewhere looking at her. Itching to lay his filthy hands on twenty thousand dollars. But he hadn't the guts to emerge from his lair. Those were her thoughts.

She was right.

Hidden away in a four-storied hotel room on David Rose Street was a man named Mohan Basdeo. The room that he rented enabled him to envision Caneview Avenue and Greenheart Street. From behind a dark curtain, he fixed his gaze on every object on the street with a smoldering eye. He saw that the woman he was supposed to meet had company. Plainclothes cops from the Georgetown Police Department. Their presence forced him to unrelent. They dampened his implacability as dull red anger gathered in his brain, waiting to explode.

He fought for self control in the tiny 10x10 room with only a table, a chair and a queen-size bed. But he had no intention of going on Caneview Avenue and dealing with the cops. He was stubbornly aware that Georgetown Police were not like the cops in New York City who read a guy his rights when making an arrest and remained calm and cool. Not so in Georgetown. That practice was taboo. Tell a cop that you have no intention of answering any of his questions or you wanted to see your attorney. And guess what! You just bought yourself a ticket to the greatest ass-kicking you have ever experienced.

With that in mind, the man resolved to stay in the comfort of the Palm Tree Hotel. The undercover woman threaded her way back to the police cruiser.

Later in the evening, another unmarked cruiser rolled up on Caneview Avenue. A police lieutenant clad in street clothes approached the surveillance car.

"Any luck?"

"Not yet," answered the big sergeant.

"I'll get someone to take the undercover back to headquarters. Meanwhile we'll keep a watch on that corner till daybreak. If the cockroach shows his face, grab his ass and put him in handcuffs. If he does not show, retrieve the bag from the garbage pail. Any questions?"

"You've covered it all, Lieutenant."

"OK. I'll see you all in the morning."

News that the man did not show up in South Ruimveldt Gardens stunned Nadira. She felt her energy sapping. Emotionally, she was unable to bear that ordeal. How could all those things be happening after just returning for a short stay to the country she loved? Why did her life evolve to such a horrible reality? She struggled for sanity.

Three days later, Nadira Gobin's cell phone rang. She felt strangely semi-present as she answered it. It was a man's voice. Venomous and haughty. She did exactly as the cops said.

"Hello."

"OK. You mutt. You were there with the cops after all!"

"I put the money in the pail for you. I stood at the corner but didn't see you."

"You're a lying slut. The cops were there with you and that means your husband won't come home."

"Why? You promised."

"Ma'am you are the one who broke your promise."

"Please. Don't hurt my husband. I'll bring you the money at any place you want. Those people who came to South Ruimveldt Gardens with me were my friends."

"But I told you to come alone."

"Mister, I don't have a car. So I had to get someone to drive me. Let me give you the money. You turn my husband loose and it all will be over."

"I'll call you in a couple of days and instruct you where to drop the money. No shit this time, OK."

"Mister, you can rely on me."

The man ended the call as Nadira sat in the kitchen with her sister and brother-in-law.

Ten minutes later the phone rang again. That time it was the police. As per arrangement, they bugged Nadira's phone in an attempt to get a general position of the mysterious caller.

"We got a cell phone signal from the vicinity of Austin and Hadfield Streets in Newburg," a policeman said.

"Thank you," Nadira responded.

"A patrol car was dispatched to the area with a GPS. We will know exactly where that phone is and who is using it if he's still there."

A week passed.

The unknown person did not make contact with Nadira Gobin. It was as if he knew he was being watched. Brickdam sleuths were in for the long haul. They figured the man they were dealing with was way above the everyday street level hood they encountered on the job.

Nadira Gobin reported her husband as a missing person to the U.S. Embassy in Georgetown.

CHAPTER 6

Six weeks passed since Cyril Gobin's flight landed at Cheddi Jagan International Airport. And it was as though he vanished into thin air. Georgetown Police detectives were getting frustrated as their efforts to find the man remained gloomy.

Two men who had criminal backgrounds were detained by police. They lived in neighboring Stevedor Housing Scheme close to the designated drop point in South Ruimveldt Gardens. Police said they were persons of interest, connected with the disappearance of Cyril Gobin, a U.S. citizen and former Guyanese national.

A confidential informant told detectives that he saw one of the men loitering on Caneview Avenue in close proximity to Greenheart Street. After hours of interrogation at Police Headquarters, both men were released owing to lack of credible evidence.

Meanwhile, Nadira's son and his family and other extended family members flew in from New York. She told the family that she had not spoken to her husband since the day he landed in Guyana. But she continued to pin her hopes on prayers.

But three days later, news media like the voice of Guyana Radio and NCN Channels 8, 11 and 25 aired an emergency call to police. The newscast pointed out that four boys with their dog went fishing in a canal off Toucan Street, adjoining

Le Repentir Cemetery. The dog found what appeared to be a T-shirt covered with dried blood. The boys said the T-shirt was partially hidden at the base of a sandbox tree.

Police cruisers with sirens ablaze bolted to the scene. The area where the shirt was located was cordoned off.

A cadaver dog was brought in from Eve Leary Police Academy. After training, the animal acquired a stupendous ability to find human remains. Its well-honed nose was programmed to detect the faint traces of the chemicals emitted by a human body during decomposition.

The officers handling the dog followed him on a ten-foot leash. Quickly the canine battled forward. Blazing a path between tall trees and shrubbery and leaving a hurried trail among elephant grass and ferns. The dog made its way to a sandbox tree. Sniffing, whining, scratching, digging. It's bark grew bitter then changed to drawling plaintive clamor.

Suddenly the canine turned on its heels. As if retracing its steps. The animal paused at the top of a small knoll. Its eyes searching the landscape as if looking for a signature that appeared nowhere else in nature. Again the dog barked as if expressing sentiments of aggravation, rage, excitement. It glinted to its left and right and suddenly it glissaded down the hill. The legs of the police officer pistoned wildly in his laboring attempts to keep up with the dog. Beyond a hollow, blacksage, monkey-apple and baby jamoon trees grew wide apart. The ground cover was dense with the abundance of guinea and coastal Bermuda grass. The dog bustled ahead, not even slowing. But suddenly without warning it decreased its speed and stopped within inches of the hollow. The animal barked and scratched with wild erratic movements. Its attention focused on one area by the hollow.

Quickly the police officer whipped out his walkie-talkie.

"Hey fellows. I think our dog found something."

"Are you kiddin' us, Officer Wiltshire?" the police corporal answered.

"I kid you not. I think Bruno, our dog, is on to something."

Quickly about five ranks raced to the scene. The area was secured and a perimeter was setup. Within thirty minutes an excavation crew showed up from Brickdam. Detectives and uniformed policemen commenced their investigation of the scene, looking for physical clues, as opening what appeared to be a shallow grave begin. Minutes passed. A faint odor of decaying flesh was apparent in the air. The digging continued and the odor became more pungent and intense.

"Lieutenant, there's a body here!" one policeman shouted.

The lieutenant plodded from his cruiser. He held a handkerchief to his nostrils. He watched as the crew unearthed a decaying corpse from a shallow grave. The body was clad in a blue T-shirt. The words New York Mets were written in front.

The pathologist was summoned to the crime scene. Accompanied by members of the Guyana Crime Lab. Position of the body, its clothing, gender and race were noted. Multiple pictures were also taken. Finally the body was bagged and transported to the office of the pathologist for an autopsy.

Meanwhile news were all over Georgetown. Police had discovered the body of a man in Le Repentir Cemetery buried in a shallow grave.

The tidings came to Subryanville. It scurried along Burchell Street and made its way to Lot 135.

Inside a woman paced the floor. Waves of impatience had produced stress lines on her brow. The people around her licked their lips and swallowed dryly, as swarms of butterflies encroached on their stomachs.

"I must call the police again!" the woman blared as a cloud of impatience kept creeping in her voice.

"Ma. You called the police already," her son responded, "at least three times."

"Nadira, remember the medical examiner and the police said they have to identify the body," her sister joined in. "They said it will take a couple of days. At this time, no one knows who it is. It may not even be Cyril."

"I don't think so, Angela," Nadira said with a constricted voice as a sudden spasm of anxiety lingered in her gut. "I have this feeling that came to me last night that Cyril is dead."

"No, no, Nadira," Kishore her brother-in-law said. "You should not say things unless you know them to be true."

"That's alright, Uncle Kishore," Nadira's son joined in. "Let Ma express her feelings. It may help her to deal with her present situation."

"I have to agree with you," Kishore responded.

Two days later the pathologist concluded his post mortem examination of the body found in a Georgetown cemetery. The report stated that the victim was buried in a shallow grave about seven weeks ago, after death, by a gunshot wound to his chest. He was of Indo-Guyanese descent, about five feet ten inches tall and weighing approximately one hundred and ninety seven pounds.

A receipt was located in one of the corpse's pockets. Police determined that the victim had stopped to eat at a Ruby Tuesday restaurant on Fifth Avenue in the City of New York. Authorities input information on the receipt in their computers. They found out that a man named Cyril Gobin used his debit card to purchase a rack of baby back ribs, French fries, vegetables and a bottle of Corona beer. That was about 3:00 p.m. on the day of his flight from New York to Georgetown.

The pathologist delivered the bullet he retrieved from the dead man's chest cavity to the police lab. He told investigators according to gun powder on the victim's shirt and burnt marks on his chest, the shot was fired from close range. Technicians determined in their forensic department that the slug came from a .38 caliber revolver.

A police cruiser was dispatched to 135 Burchell Street in Subryanville to have the family identify the body.

CHAPTER 7

The funeral was small and solitary at the Ferraria Brothers Funeral Home on Charlotte Street in Georgetown. Entirely different from the funeral they had two days ago. A police officer, killed in the line of duty. Cars and people crowded the street from the Supreme Court building to Wellington and Robb Streets.

The Gobin family boarded a couple of limousines after last rites were performed by a pundit, an Indo-Guyanese priest. The casket was closed. No one was permitted to view the body because of its advanced state of decomposition. The limousines traveled slowly behind the hearse carrying the remains as it made a left turn on Russell Street towards Houston Access Road. Half a dozen cars followed the procession.

Ahead of that convoy of vehicles was a 1995 Ford Explorer. On its roof, a blue light was flashing, heralding other vehicles to make way for the moving procession. Two men sat in the unmarked sports utility truck. They were attired as if they were going on a cruise to the Cayman Islands. But on the contrary, the duo were Eve Leary sleuths, assigned to investigate the abduction and murder of Cyril Gobin.

The driver, the younger of the two men, had a thin, craggy, Indo-Guyanese face, with black, gun-metal eyes and dark brown hollows for cheekbones. When he spoke, his lips rolled back, exposing well-set, glistening white teeth.

"Ever wonder why the Gobins want to bury in Grove and not elsewhere?" the driver asked after a long silence.

"Remember, the man was born and raised in Grove. Maybe the family sees this as a homecoming of sorts," the other man said. He was Afro-Guyanese, about fifty-two and a police force veteran for twenty-two years. His leathery complexion gave way to the passage of time. Yet his chiseled, charismatic face and steady but yet warm eye contact brought him through the ranks from constable to lead detective.

"That's understandable. Besides, I guess the family was against putting him in a cemetery where he was found murdered."

"Now you're talking."

"Must be a difficult experience for a family. Guy coming to Guyana to visit his people and ends up biting the dust."

"One thing we all have to remember, that is everyone will go back to his maker someday, sometime," the lead detective responded as his muddy, dark brown eyes were focused on the highway. "Could be today, tomorrow or whenever."

"You're scaring the crap out of me, Martin."

"Nothing to be scared of man. It's biology."

"That's the reason I dislike funerals."

"Why? Because you think death is scary."

"No. Paying respects to the dead should be something both personal and private. Not a ritual that borders on a public spectacle."

"To each his own, Alan."

"True. But look at our fellow cop who was buried two days ago in Georgetown. The entire affair exceeded my threshold for melancholy. The satiating perfume of a sea of flowers and faces distorted by grief and pain are things that are not easy to forget."

"In this job there's no thresholds for anything. As a cop you're supposed to expect the unexpected. That frame of mind always got me through difficult situations. It will do the same for you. Including keeping you alive."

"Wouldn't question that."

The Ford Explorer rolled through the towns of Prospect and Little Diamond and then through Big Diamond. A brief silence ensued between the men as the vehicle headed towards the township of Grove. Its driver was a cop named Alan Ramsammy, in his mid-thirties with eight years of law enforcement under his belt. Five years as a constable patrolling the streets of Port Mourant, Corentyne and three years later as a detective in Georgetown. The Explorer crossed the Big Jimbo Bridge as the funeral procession continued in tow.

A half mile ahead, the vehicle made a right on a dirt road and into the Grove Township Cemetery. Sandbox trees with their thorny trunks loomed as if reaching for the clouds. They stood in clustered formations, silent and august, like zombies in a horror picture show. Then the sudden resounding cry of a jackdaw came from the leafy boughs of a giant immortelle tree. A piercing and unabated clamor as if proclaiming the harbinger of a great evil. The noise stopped as suddenly as it began.

The two limousines and a couple of cars pulled past the Explorer when it came to a side road and stopped. People swarmed out of the vehicles. By then the hearse had already gone into position by an opened grave.

"Stay in the truck, Alan," Martin Brogan, the lead detective said to his sidekick as he exited the vehicle. "I'll go by the graveside and show my face." So saying Brogan made his police badge visible on the left side of his shirt.

"OK, Martin."

"Remember, keep your eyes peeled. Watch for anyone acting suspicious and observe cars that didn't come with the convoy."

"Sure."

"Why is that, Alan?"

"Simple. Some killers have an obsessive compulsive mind-set. They get a high just to see families of their victims suffer."

"You got that right Alan. You nailed that right on the head. Watch my back."

"OK."

Before Martin Brogan reached the graveside, four young brawny men removed the body from the hearse in an unadorned wooden coffin, with handles made of brass. They lay it by the graveside. Again a pundit was on the scene, officiating rites that were compassionately brief. Martin

Brogan watched from behind a small group of people. Mostly men.

One of the mourners, a middle-aged Indo-Guyanese woman with flowing ebony hair and dressed in black, was at the point of collapse. Brogan's probing eyes saw her being helped to the front seat of a parked limousine as her weeping and wailing continued. A man in his early thirties with a face growing haggard with worry was trying to comfort her. He closed the vehicle's door and maneuvered back to the graveside. As he passed Brogan, he flashed him an inquisitive look as if wondering who he was. But quickly his expression changed when he saw Brogan's police badge.

The man turned on his heels and approached Brogan with smoldering eyes.

"You're a cop. Are you not?" he asked Brogan.

"Yes. The name's Martin Brogan. I'm the chief detective assigned to this investigation. My partner, Alan Ramsammy, is in the police vehicle over there. What's your name?"

"I'm Winston Gobin, son of the deceased."

"Mr. Gobin. I want to express my sorrow to you and your family for the loss of your father. Indeed it was heart-wrenching."

"Yes, Officer, thank you for your concern. Such events, one can never be prepared for."

"You can bet on that."

"Well, let me go check on my mother in the limousine."

"Before you go, take my card," Brogan said diving into his pocket. "Give this card to your mother. Tell her to call me if she hears or sees anything. Or if anyone tries to contact her."

"I will do that for sure, Officer."

Thirty minutes passed.

Brogan shrinked away in silence from the graveside and got into the Explorer.

"Any luck?" Ramsammy was the first to speak.

"I talked to the dead man's son. I gave him my card to pass on to his mother."

"I guess that was his mother in the limo who was sobbing."

"Yes."

The gravediggers were hard at work when the Ford Explorer made a left turn on the East Bank Highway. It headed due north through a densely populated section of town, not very far from the cemetery, where most of the deceased would be buried. Inevitably laying claim to a lasting piece of Grove Township's real estate.

CHAPTER 8

Police Headquarters, Brickdam.

The coming weeks found Martin Brogan and his partner sifting through evidence that was recovered from the crime scene. A cigarette butt was examined for fingerprints and DNA by the crime lab. The results were in. There were no hits in the police database.

"Looks like we back to square one, Martin," Alan Ramsammy said.

"We never got off square one. Our closest contact with that bastard was during his call to Nadira Gobin."

"Maybe he was never arrested or doesn't have a criminal record."

"No. If he was, we would have gotten our man. Brickdam finger prints everyone who is arrested."

"Looks like a dead end is looming."

"I wouldn't say so. We got to find this guy whoever he is. I strongly believe he might have murdered more people."

"That may be true. But for two weeks we have fanned out the streets. From Roxanne Burnham Gardens to Palm Road in South Ruimveldt. Nobody seems to know anything."

"Detective work takes time, Alan. Nothing just happens overnight. You got to stay the course if you want results doing this kinda work."

"Guess you're right. Just a little anxious."

"It happens to the best."

"What's our next move?"

"Let's go back to the time when the cat called Nadira Gobin with her husband's cell phone. We got to assume that the perpetrator had either already murdered Cyril Gobin or the victim was severely incapacitated."

"Point taken. That's how he was able to get the phone," Ramsammy answered.

"Right. A man isn't just going to give up his shit, just like that."

"No, he's gonna fight."

"So the jitterbug called the man's wife to say he needed money before the man can come home. She agreed to deliver money to the low-life but turned around and called the cops anyway."

"I know the rest Martin. When she showed with the money our man never came forward to collect."

"That's true. But why he refused to pick up the twenty grand he demanded?"

"That son-of-a-bitch might have been somewhere in hiding nearby when he thought he saw Nadira Gobin with cops in unmarked cars," Alan Ramsammy concluded.

"During that stakeout, the police did not see any strange vehicle."

"I don't think he was hiding in one of the homes on Caneview Avenue or Greenheart Street. We spoke to those residents. They saw nothing."

"Hey, what about that four-storied hotel on David Rose Street? The Palm Tree Hotel. We didn't check that place."

"You're right, Martin. He could have been in a room somewhere in that hotel."

"Well, what are we waiting for. Let's go over there right now."

"Good idea man. You know I'm with you on this."

Quickly the men got into the Ford Explorer. That time it was Martin Brogan who sat in the driver's seat. He placed the key into the ignition and turned the key. The engine started, convulsed and suddenly died. Martin hit the key again. That time the 5.0-liter V8 engine roared from within its compartment. It was music to Martin Brogan's ear.

"Looks like this vehicle needs a tune-up," Alan Ramsammy said as he gave Martin Brogan an ironic stare.

"Could be right. A vehicle three years old and I could bet my last buck, it was never tuned."

"You know what that tells you."

"What?"

"Transport has been sittin' on their balls doing nothing. Just getting' fat."

"That's what they say about all public sector jobs. Government workers sit on their butts and collect taxpayers money without lifting a darn finger."

"Not like that with this job man."

"I know so."

The vehicle traveled southeast on Brickdam Street, then it made a right turn by Square of the Revolution onto Hadfield Street. It moved through Lodge, East La Penitence and East Ruimveldt to Mandela Avenue. Within minutes it stopped in front of the Palm Tree Hotel on David Rose

Street. The detectives piled out of their truck and ambled along a walkway leading to the hotel's main entrance.

It was about 1:30 p.m. in early May. The sky was blue. A punishing heat reigned down from an oppressive sun when Martin Brogan and his partner opened the door of the Palm Tree Hotel.

A Chinese woman sat at a front desk working on invoices as two Amer-Indian women pushed a linen cart down a hallway.

"May I assist you men?" the woman asked as she studied the men with a quiet acuteness.

"I am Martin Brogan and this is Officer Alan Ramsammy. We both are from the Georgetown Police Department," the lead detective said showing politeness as he approached the woman and displaying his badge. "What's your name, ma'am? Are you the owner of this establishment?"

"Yes, Officer. I'm the owner. My name is Pauline Yhap. What can I do for you today?"

"There has been a kidnapping and murder of a Guyanese returning to Georgetown from New York on holiday."

"How awful! I'm sorry to hear that, Officer. It seems as though Georgetown is getting more dangerous by the minute. But what can I do to help you?"

"We got reason to believe, ma'am, that a person of interest related to our investigation may have rented a room and stayed here for a couple of hours," Alan Ramsammy chimed in.

"What? How preposterous. When did this happen?"

"About mid-March. Would you care if we were to check your guest register?" Martin Brogan said.

"Not at all. It's here. Let's check," the woman said as she reached under a counter and came out with a guest register book. "You said it was in March."

"Yes. About mid-March," Ramsammy said.

"On March 13, a man alone rented Room 405, on the fourth floor," the woman said as she examined the guest register.

"What's his name and what was the registration and description of his vehicle?" Martin Brogan asked.

"His name according to what he wrote here is Phillip Mangar. The vehicle was a brown minibus with a registration of HZM 489."

"Interesting. How long was he here?" Ramsammy asked.

"He checked in at 7:00 p.m. and left at 11:00 p.m." the woman said.

"You mind if we check the room?" Martin Brogan asked.

"Not at all. The room is not occupied at this moment. I'll take you there."

The woman and the two lawmen walked up four flights of stairs. They tottered along a hallway until they came to Room 405. The woman who said her name was Pauline Yhap opened the door. The group stumbled into the room, as a fierce undeniable smell of tobacco hung stubbornly in the air.

"This is the room Mr. Mangar rented on March 13, about two months ago."

"Had you rented this room to anyone since then?" Martin Brogan asked the woman who wore a blue frumpy and shapeless dress far bigger than her lean, scrawny frame.

"Yes," the woman answered, "on at least six occasions. Couples showed up, rented the room, stay for five or six hours and left."

Then Alan Ramsammy walked over to some heavy green drapery. He pulled a cord and exposed a double set of windows overlooking Caneview Avenue and Greenheart Street. It depicted a straight path to the intersection of the two streets. And a black metal garbage pail designed for the street was in full view from the window.

"Martin, check this out, partner!"

"What did you see?"

"Look at the garbage pail over there."

"Yes. I know what you're saying. Our man was in this room watching the woman he thought was Mrs. Gobin and the undercover cops as she delivered the package."

"No wonder he didn't swallow the bait. He saw the cops out there."

"Yes, indeed. He had the drop on them."

"That's for sure, Martin. What's next boss?" Alan Ramsammy asked.

"We gotta pay the Department of Motor Vehicles a visit, young man."

Martin Brogan thanked the hotel owner for her kindness. Then he and his partner blazed a trail back to Brickdam Street. Their objective, the motor vehicle headquarters.

It was 3:00 p.m. when Martin Brogan and his partner walked in the office of the assistant director. He was a middle-aged, wide-hipped man with a despairing look and a megaphonic voice.

"Hey, Martin Brogan. Haven't seen you and your buddy around here in a while," the man said as he grabbed the detectives' hands and shook them with claw-like fingers.

"That's true, Galloway. Haven't been around here in years," Martin Brogan said.

"The street hoods keep us busy," Alan said.

"I know that, Ramsammy. It's getting bad everywhere in Georgetown," Tony Galloway said.

"That's the reason we're here," Brogan said. "We're trying to solve a murder."

"It's a minibus owner. He may be our man," Alan Ramsammy said. "Here's the particulars."

Tony Galloway took the notebook with the particulars and sat by his computer. He entered the information into the motor vehicle data bank. After a few seconds he shook his head greenly and looked up at the detectives.

"No dice guys. There's nothing here matching that registration."

"What do you mean, Tony? Are you kiddin' us?" Martin Brogan said giving a start of surprise.

"Am I hearing right?" Alan Ramsammy asked, as a rush of heat enveloped his face.

"It's right here guys. That registration cannot be found. It's a fake."

"What about the name Phillip Mangar? Input that name and let's see if that person owns a minibus," Brogan said.

Galloway typed in the name Phillip Mangar. Four such names came up in the screen. One man lived in Crabwood Creek on the Corentyne coast. He was the owner of a Toyota Corolla. The other Phillip Mangar resided in Belladrum on the west coast of Berbice. He was the owner of a Mercedes Benz 280C. The third Phillip Mangar was the owner of a LandRover Defender 110 series and the final Phillip Mangar, residing in Lenora on the west coast of Demerara, had a Grand Cherokee Limited.

"You see guys, the man you're looking for may have given a false name and registration when he checked in at the hotel," Tony Galloway said.

"We've been through this before," Brogan answered.

"True. But it is unnerving," Ramsammy added.

"The man you guys are looking for may be a witty criminal," Galloway said.

"That's true. He may also be an everyday fellow who drives a brown minibus for a living," Alan Ramsammy said.

The two men left the department of motor vehicles about 4:30 p.m. that evening. They headed back to Brickdam Street.

"What's your plan for tomorrow, Martin?" Ramsammy asked.

"We got to talk to the four Mangar guys and find out what they know."

"OK."

"Go home man, Alan. Get some sleep. We'll start again in the morning."

CHAPTER 9

Nadira Gobin was alone and adrift like a solitary cloud as she sat in her sister's house in Subryanville. In her mind, there existed a tiny concept of time, in the months following her husband's murder. She remembered the cotton-draped coffin of a man who had dared to dream of a new existence beyond the shores of Guyana. A brighter future and then a dramatic end in a place and time no one expected.

But Nadira Gobin wanted to be philosophical about her husband's demise. Five months have passed and her melancholy had reduced her to a woman with a fierce, droopy face. Then she realized that a human's life was small, fragile and finite. And yet so laden with splendor. She got from her chair and went into the bathroom with mincing footsteps. She splashed water on her face. It was 8:00 p.m. that evening. Kishore and Angela had been offering her rum and cream soda after dinner. They insisted that she have a drink despite her indignation. Eventually she gave in.

She eyed herself in the mirror. Jet black hair, a button nose and reddened, sullen eyes.

Then her cell phone rang.

Her face hardened for a quick second as she turned toward the phone sitting on her vanity. Her eyes stayed on the phone for a long moment. It rang. She swallowed hard before taking it up to answer.

"Hello. Who is this?"

"It's me, Nadira. Cyril's friend."

"You bastard! Where did you get my name?"

"On Cyril's phone. I know you're his wife. I'm not that dumb."

"I discontinued Cyril's phone. It's shut off. You murdered my husband! The cops are after you."

"I threw away Cyril's phone. I'm calling from a public phone. Let the police catch me if they can."

"What do you want from me?"

"Money!"

"I have no money. You dog."

"You better look out lady. I'll be coming to get you too. I hope you got someone watching your back. I know where you're staying."

Then the man hung up the phone.

Nadira closed her cell phone and called her sister and brother-in-law. Angela and her husband Kishore swooped into her room.

"The man who killed Cyril just called me again!" Nadira Gobin was able to say. Her voice constricted. Her face a mask of terror.

"What!" Kishore Saroop exclaimed. "You did discontinue Cyril's phone. I know you did."

"Yes," Nadira sobbed, "he said he was calling from a public phone and he was coming to get me. Just as he did my husband!"

"I know the police must have heard him. Because your phone is bugged," Angela said.

"True," Nadira said as her stomach fluttered.

Then Nadira's phone rang again.

She picked it up with trembling hands as her eyes welled up with tears.

"Hello. Is this Nadira Gobin?"

It was a woman's voice. Soft and reassuring.

"Yes. This is she."

"Mrs. Gobin, this is Officer McGee from the Police Department. We are monitoring your phone to keep track of the man who had been calling you."

"He called about fifteen minutes ago," Nadira said, her knees quaking. "He wanted money. And said he knows where I live and was coming to kill me."

"We have that on record, Mrs. Gobin."

"So what next?"

"A police cruiser is patrolling your street as we speak. Stay indoors. This individual may be armed and dangerous."

"This is insane," Nadira said as she felt a chill running up her spine. "Whoever that man is, he's not going to scare me or run me out of Guyana. I was born here and I'm not leaving until he's arrested for killing my husband."

"We the police are working hard to catch him. Tomorrow the detective assigned to investigate your husband's disappearance and murder will pay you a visit."

"OK, Officer."

The following day about 10:30 a.m. the Ford Explorer pulled to a stop at 135 Burchell Street in Subryanville. Martin Brogan exited the vehicle. He was alone. Alan Ramsammy had the day off. His resolute footsteps moved his six-foot frame with a stately carriage. He rang the doorbell. Twice. Angela opened the door.

"I'm Detective Brogan."

"Nice meeting you detective. I saw you at the cemetery in Grove Township at Cyril's funeral."

"You must be Mrs. Gobin's sister."

"Yes. I am Angela Saroop. I live here with my husband Kishore. Please come in."

"Is Nadira around?"

"Yes, she's stepping out the shower."

"I'll wait till she gets out."

"Sure. Have a seat here Detective."

"Thanks."

So saying, Angela Saroop, a small and dainty woman with a long blue dress and seaweed brown eyes and a roguish smile, disappeared in an adjoining room.

Martin Brogan sat in a sofa. The hard mahogany wood that covered the first floor gleamed beneath slants of sunlight from an opened window. A subtle smell of incense lingered in the air. Two light brown love seats flanked a half-moon table. Wooden figurines of antbears, turtles and other animals decorated its top. Across the floor, there was a deep overstuffed sofa. A small reading table piled high with books and newspaper stood beside the chair.

Suddenly Nadira Gobin came down a flight of stairs with a catlike grace. She was attired in a light yellow tent dress. Voluminous with no waistline. Her feet were decorated by flat leather sandals with straps separating the first and second toes.

"Good morning, Detective. I hope you weren't waiting long," Nadira said. Her face fresh but her eyes gave way to a wounded look. Brogan stood up. "Good morning to you too, ma'am." She toddled towards him with opened arms. Quickly he reached out and pulled her close to him. Her face an expression of mute appeal. Her lean, petite body touching his. He gazed into her burnt-almond eyes. They were soft, vulnerable, tender but yet tantalizing. Then she unwrapped her hands from around him and sat in a nearby chair. Her body wash of Victoria Secret Strawberries and Champagne permeated the air.

"So we did get a report that you got another call," Martin Brogan said.

"Yes. Two days ago a man called me. It's the same man who I think killed Cyril."

"We have that information. But what was he saying?"

"He wanted me to give him money."

"The man's a psychopath."

"Not only that. He said he will kill me as he killed my husband."

"That's just talk."

"I have to take it serious, Detective. I'm now a widow. I do not carry a gun so I am afraid of this man. He said he knows where I'm living."

"I understand your concern. We are trying our best to apprehend this man."

"He said he was speaking to me from a public phone. Where was that phone situated, Detective? Do you know?"

"In Soesdyke. After the call was made to your phone, which we have under surveillance, we noted that it was made not too far from the airport."

"Really."

"Indeed. So we sent a police cruiser to where the phone is located."

"Did you see the man?"

"No. He was gone. But we were able to lift some prints from the phone."

"Is that so?"

"Yes. And guess what? The prints matched those we found on a cigarette butt at Le Repentir Cemetery where your husband was buried."

"What. Looks like you're getting closer to this guy."

"Maybe."

"Detective. Can I offer you some coffee? Maybe your wife made you a cup earlier but another cup will not hurt."

"Sure, thank you. But I'm not married, ma'am. At least not anymore."

"Divorced?"

"Yes. Six years ago."

"Sorry to hear that, Detective."

"Thank you. But it's a part of life."

"That's so true. Any children?"

"Yes. A daughter."

"Is she living with you?"

"No. She left the country with her mother years ago."

"I know you're dying to see her. How old is she?"

"She's twenty-one now and you bet I'll give anything to see my daughter right now."

"That's for sure. Is she in college?"

"Yes. She'll finish in a year, majoring in computer technology."

"My son graduated from New York University three years ago. He works for a big corporation."

"Was that your boy I saw at the funeral?"

"Yes. That was him. He's twenty-five."

"What a nice kid. Have any more children?"

"No, just him. He's married to one of his college friends, an African American girl."

"Hey. Nothing's wrong with that. They loved each other and they did what they had to do."

"Sadly enough, his father Cyril did not think so. He felt his son betrayed him."

"That's his opinion. What did you think?"

"I could not object. Who am I to make that determination? They have to live together."

"You like her?"

"Sure I do. I love my two grandchildren, too. They're so cute."

"That's a good attitude to have Mrs. Gobin."

"Please call me Nadira, Detective Brogan."

"OK. You can call me Martin."

"Martin, can I call you if there's a problem?"

"Sure, Nadira. Call me at anytime. It's my job to make sure you're safe."

"That's so reassuring," she answered as her face beamed fondly.

CHAPTER 10

Weeks went by.

There had been another case of a woman who did not show up in Georgetown after leaving Toronto for a short vacation in Guyana. Her body was discovered by a farmer. Police said the seventy-year-old woman's remains were found at the roadside in the town of Friendship on the East Bank of Demerara.

Police cordoned off the area situated about half a mile from the Marabunta Bridge creek.

Martin Brogan and his partner Alan Ramsammy were called to the scene. The first uniformed cops who arrived in Friendship did a good job of preserving the integrity of the crime area and minutes later the patrol supervisor stationed in Craig Village arrived. The officers did not move or touch any physical evidence. A few bystanders were prevented from encroaching on the scene.

Brogan and his partner photographed the area involved. Shots were taken from all angles and distance with a high efficiency camera. A brown paper bag and pieces of the victim's clothing found scattered over a small area were likely targets for fingerprinting. The detectives bagged the evidence for dusting.

After two hours, the pathologist arrived. A lean Chinese woman in her late sixties. Her face bore a gaunt expression as she inserted her long, delicate fingers into a pair of latex gloves. She scrutinized the corpse. It was wedged between the aerial roots of a mangrove tree and other indigenous riverside shrubbery. She made a note of the time of the day, temperature, humidity and the weather in the area in order to establish the time of death to a greater degree of accuracy.

The body was later bagged and transported to the Georgetown morgue where an autopsy was going to be performed to reveal the cause of death.

Brogan and his partner got into the Ford Explorer. They headed back to Georgetown to drop off the evidence they gathered at the police crime lab.

"This job never ceases to amaze me, Martin."

"Reckon you're right."

"Man, there's always shit going on."

"That's the nature of the beast."

"Now we're investigating three murders. And you know something. I wouldn't be surprised if one man, one piece of dog squeeze, is responsible for all these atrocities."

"Could be possible. But only evidence can prove that."

"Right."

"Tomorrow we'll come back to Friendship. You know the old routine. Find any eyewitness. Maybe someone may have seen something."

"OK, Martin. What are you doing tonight man? I'm taking my woman to the movies."

"I don't know what I'll be doing."

"What about that Gobin woman? I know she'd been after you."

"Yes. She calls me often with her sister's cell phone."

"You know what that means."

"Yes. She doesn't want anyone listening to her conversation."

"Right. She also wants to hook up with you, man. It's been six months since her husband was murdered."

"Alan, the woman is just plain lonely."

"She wants a life man, I'm sure. You've been going to clubs and stuff since your divorce. I know, to you it's boring, Martin. You need a real woman."

"True. But as far as I'm concerned, a romantic relationship with Nadira Gobin and myself will be morally and ethically inappropriate."

"Be real, Martin. Don't you think that woman gets horny sometimes?"

"Sure. At fifty-two, I want to get laid sometimes. But what about ethics?"

"Screw ethics. I'm sure the police commissioner is out there jacking up some woman who isn't his wife. Right now, I bet you."

"That's him. I wouldn't do what he does."

"But if you continue like this, Martin, what's in it for you? I know you're getting laid. There are tons of women out there. But man, you need quality, not quantity."

"She's East Indian. I'm a black man."

"Who cares about race? You and I know Martin, that Guyana is becoming a melting pot."

"Guess you're right. Maybe I'll ask her out tonight."

"She's only fifty. Right in your ballpark. Go for the gold," Alan Ramsammy said as his cheeks drew back by a nasty chuckle.

Martin Brogan responded with a lascivious laughter.

It was 4:00 p.m. when the Ford Explorer pulled in the parking lot of police headquarters on Brickdam Street.

Alan Ramsammy parked the truck for the night. Both men headed to their personal vehicles. Martin Brogan got into his 1994 Toyota Corolla. It sported a 1.6L 4-cylinder engine with a five-speed manual transmission. The engine purred when he turned on the ignition.

Then he got to thinking about Nadira Gobin. He remembered her saying that she felt safe in starting a friendship with a man who was in law enforcement. When they embraced at her sister's house, he looked into her eyes. Those burnt-almond, dew drop eyes. Rich and moist. Her face was tan, with strong Caucasian features. Being well over six feet, he towered over her diminutive frame. She was aware of his gaze creeping over her. And had no other choice but to meet his eyes. Despite his brief knowledge of her, he hadn't had a woman linger on his mind since his wife walked out on him over six years ago. He had been a happy man then, back in 1992. He remembered when Olive and him shared a small apartment in Alexander Village. They didn't know what problems were. He remembered her telling him that they were made for each other, forever. It was the afternoon when he left police headquarters. As if it were yesterday. They lay in bed, listening to a fierce thunderstorm as it hammered the tin roof.

But things changed without warning.

And for years, he made some serious attempts to sift through the ashes of a failed marriage. But his attempts were futile. Where on earth did he go wrong? The question hacked at his inside, like the fangs of an angry safari carnivore.

Then the sudden ringing of his cell phone took him out of his musings.

"Hello. Martin here."

"Martin, this is Nadira. How are you?"

"Doing fine. I see you're using the house phone. What's up with your cell?"

"Needs a new battery. It died today on me."

"That's not a problem. If you have dinner with me tonight, maybe we can pick up a new battery for your phone."

"Really. Are you serious?"

"Dead serious."

"Oh, I'll love to, Martin."

"Well, I will pick you up at eight."

"OK. Thanks."

Martin Brogan closed his phone. A demure giggle swept his countenance. He wanted to call Nadira to ask her out that night but ruled against that because her phone was bugged by the police. He could not afford to have Brickdam know that he was seeing the widow of a murder victim under his investigation. But psychic phenomenon, he figured caused her to call him and made him a believer of serendipity.

He made a left on Vlissengen Road and a right on the main road towards Cummings Lodge. The place he called home. Wedged between Liliendaal and Ogle. Traffic was the norm at that time of day. Bumper to bumper. Drivers with venomous visages regarded each other with murderous eyes. By 5:30 p.m., he pulled into his driveway. His house was a small, white, two-storied bungalow surrounded by houses of Mediterranean, Floridian and Spanish-style architecture. Brick and stucco exteriors topped with red or green roofs, fashioned with courtyards, wrought iron railings and sweeping verandas.

Martin Brogan opened his door and went to his refrigerator. He grabbed a bottle of water and quenched his thirst. Part of the first floor had enough lavender-rose wallpaper and matching fabric and furniture one could shake a stick at. Three years ago, he left Alexander Village and bought his piece of property. His interior designer was a full-figured Trinidadian woman with a sweetly expressive face but a gift to gab.

By 7:00 p.m., he quickly showered, changed into a pair of Levi jeans and a casual blue T-shirt. He called Nadira at her sister's house at 7:45 p.m. He was on his way to pick her up. Martin Brogan got to Burchell Street in Subryanville at 8:10 p.m. He found Nadira standing in the dim glow of an incandescent light on the front porch. He gazed at her candidly as she came to the car. She wore a long, loose crimson cocktail dress with floral prints. Her jet-black hair, far beyond the neckline of her sleeveless dress, dangled over her shoulders. Her mascara was subtle, like it was not there. Brogan thought she looked tantalizingly foreign.

Nadira Gobin got in the Toyota. Her eau de cologne fragrance enveloped the car. A look of bliss settled on Brogan's face.

"How are you doing? Guess I'm ten minutes late," Brogan was the first to speak.

"I'm doing fine. You're not late, Martin."

"What would you like to eat?"

"Whatever you are eating. Maybe steak or chicken. You're the boss, Martin."

"Chicken."

"Sounds good."

By eight-thirty, stars were beginning to emerge across the sky. The Toyota moved with a moderate speed as the twilight deepened. Twenty minutes later, the vehicle pulled into the parking lot of the Pegasus Hotel on Sea Wall Road in Kingston.

They got out of the car and walked to a place named Brown's Restaurant, tucked away in the lobby of the hotel. As they walked, he was aware of her peripheral gaze settling over him. She forced herself to meet his eyes. She felt comfortable, despite Cyril's death and her inner turmoil. Brogan's friendship, it appeared, helped her to deal with her harsh reality, day by day.

He flashed her a knowing, easy smile as he extended his hand and brought her close to him. She looked far younger than fifty, he thought. Her hand was soft and smooth. Her fingers tapered and well manicured. Her only jewelries were her wedding band, a pair of sterling silver, diamond circled rings in her pierced ears and a matching pendant.

They moved towards the door in a loose-boned gait, inhaling the fresh night air as the roaring waves of the Atlantic Ocean crashed and convulsed against the shore.

The sound of a steady music from the inside could be heard. Brogan opened the door. The voice of Cab Calloway III, an African-American jazz singer and bandleader encompassed the atmosphere with a faint whisper. When the CD came to an end, it was replaced by the voice of Dick Johnson, a famous rhythm and blues singer.

The crowd was moderate. Couples eating, talking and laughing.

A young woman, with a short hip-hugger skirt and black fish-net stockings met them a short distance from the door.

"Good evening," she said.

"Good evening," Martin Brogan answered.

"Just two in your party?"

"Yes," Brogan answered again.

"Any special seating?"

"No," Brogan said.

"OK. Follow me."

They followed the young woman along a red-carpeted floor to a vacant table. The interior of the club was elaborate. Polished mahogany walls, cathedral ceilings decorated by crystal Tiffany chandeliers.

"Here you are," the woman said as she placed a pair of menus on the table. "Your waitress will be with you shortly."

"Thank you," Nadira Gobin said.

Martin Brogan pulled a chair from the table and allowed Nadira to be seated. Then he sat opposite her.

A few minutes later a waitress showed up.

"Are we ready to order?"

"Yes," Nadira said.

She ordered fried chicken with a scoop of white rice and a small order of dholl with fried calaloo. Brogan ordered the same dish.

"Do you like dholl, Martin?"

"Of course. It's my culture. I grew up eating dholl and rice. My mother used to cook dholl often when we lived in Bagotstown."

"Interesting. I cook dholl a lot when I'm in New York. Will you like me to cook you some?"

"I will love that."

When dinner was finished, they drank wine. A couple of people were dancing on a polished floor not far from the bar. The song "Lady in Red" by Chris DeBurgh was playing from a CD. It came softly through the ceiling speakers. Nadira looked across at him, and he knew what he had to do. Brogan reached across the table. She held his hand as they both got up slowly and slinked towards the dance floor. As he held her, he experienced a surge, like an electrical charge running through his body. They embraced on the floor. Two imperfect halves had then become a perfect whole. Like a butterfly in a cocoon. He sensed her smell. A combination of perfume, heat and her hair. At times, she flashed him a gaze. Her face, a picture of delight. Her lips parted in a gracious smile. And ever so slowly, they gyrated to the music in a slow, deliberate pace. He almost closed his eyes as she lay her head on his chest. Her ear pressed against his heart. She felt it beat. And during that moment, to her, nothing in the world had any meaning. Not going back to New York nor the psychopath who was focused on harassing the life out of her. All that was meaningful, was that moment.

By 11:45 p.m., the pair left the Pegasus. They drove home on Sea Wall Road, only to hear the crashing of the waves against the breakwater and to smell the salty fragrance of the Atlantic crosswinds. Nadira inched closer to Martin Brogan. She ran her fingers slowly and gently over his forearm in the quiet of the car.

"I enjoyed myself tonight, Nadira," he said.

"I had a good time too," she said just as he had anticipated she would say. "But aren't you going to invite me to your house, Martin?"

"Sure," he said. "I will love to show you where I live."

She responded with a radiant smile.

The vehicle shot past Subryanville then through Liliendaal until it came to Cummings Lodge. When it reached 142 Carlton Street, it pulled into the driveway.

"Here we go. This is my nest."

"It's beautiful, Martin. Nice bungalow."

"Thanks."

Brogan activated the garage door from his car and pulled inside. They made their way from the garage to the first floor. He hit the switch. A single circular florescent light cast its bright glow everywhere.

"Make yourself at home," Brogan said.

"Thanks for the invitation. May I borrow your phone, Martin? I want to call Angela."

"Sure. It's on the wall over there."

Nadira walked past a little coffee table decorated by a small lamp. A medium-sized sofa stood in front of it.

On top of a china cabinet lay a tiny collection of books. She got to the kitchen where a wall phone hung by a small microwave.

Nadira took the phone off the receiver and dialed her sister.

"Hello, this is Angela."

"Angela, this is your sister."

"Are you having a good time?"

"Sure. We went to the Pegasus. We dined and danced. It was great fun."

"What time are you coming home? It's about 12:30 a.m."

"I'll stay over at Martin's house tonight. He is right here in Cummings Lodge. He has a bungalow on Carlton Street."

"How nice. I know the area."

"I am enjoying myself."

"That's the way to go, Nadira. You were through enough."

"Thanks. I'll see you and Kishore tomorrow."

"OK."

Nadira hung up the phone and walked towards the kitchen. Brogan knew she called her sister but was unaware of what was said. He got a bottle of beer from the refrigerator and popped it open.

"Let me show you the rest of the house."

"Sure, I'm ready."

They ascended a stairway and came to the second floor. There were two bedrooms. The master had a king-sized bed with a Royal Velvet comforter set and accessories. The wallpaper was off-white with subtle images of tulips and day lilies. A moderate Jacuzzi with a shower and toilet were in a self-contained bathroom.

The guest bedroom was not so embellished. It sported a queen-sized bed, covered by a Mainstay Octagon quilt. The walls were painted with a semi-gloss eggshell latex and decorated by pictures of flowers, birds and animals.

"How gorgeous, Martin. I'm falling in love with your house."

"Glad you're loving it."

He put his beer on the vanity and walked towards her. On her face he saw an expression that was telling him she wanted him as badly as he wanted her. He mildly pulled her towards him. Running his hands in her long hair. Baked by the sun till it was tawny. He kissed her deeply. With everything he was able to muster. Her soft whispers of satisfaction fell gently on his ears. They propelled him to slide his arms around her. He kissed her cheeks, her nose and her neck. Then turned to her lips again. They walked with a voluptuous sway back to the master bedroom. Almost still entwined. Then he led her quietly to his bed.

She didn't resist.

Both disrobed in haste and whispered words of endearment in each other's ears.

CHAPTER 11

It was 9:45 a.m. the following day. Both Nadira Gobin and Martin Brogan were rudely awakened by the ringing of Brogan's cell phone.

"Hello," Brogan answered.

"Martin. This is Alan."

"Alan. What time is it?"

"It's nearly ten. You're supposed to meet me at the office at nine."

"Damn, I'm late. Must have overslept."

"No big deal partner. When will I see you?"

"Give me an hour. I'll be down there."

Brogan ended the call and looked over at Nadira. Her beady eyes regarded Brogan as if bemoaned by sleep. Her face still radiant with good cheer.

"Did I get you in trouble, Martin?"

"No. Not in the least. Just a little late for work."

"You can go. I'll stay at your house till you get back this evening."

"That's nice of you," he said as he reached over and kissed her.

"I'll cook you dinner."

"Good idea. What you'll cook me?"

"Whatever you got in the house."

"OK. I have to get moving."

"Martin, where's the TV control?"

"In that draw."

Quickly he went into the bathroom. When he was dressed, he made coffee and offered her a cup in bed. He caressed her and gazing at her fondly, he quickly left.

Within half hour he reached his office on Brickdam Road. Alan Ramsammy shot him a conspiratorial gesture when he opened the door.

"Dude, did I disturb anything?"

"No. I'm glad you called. I was fast asleep," Brogan answered as his face cracked into an angelic smile.

"There you go. I suspected you had company."

"Sure. I invited the lady out last night."

"Where did you hang out?"

"At the Pegasus. Had dinner, wine, dancing. Nadira decided to spend the night at my place."

"I had a feeling she was with you. You never show up late for work."

"Sometimes a man's gotta do what a man's gotta do."

"You're a lucky dog, Martin."

"Well, I wish I had some luck finding our man. It's long overdue."

"True. All we need is a break."

"We've got to get going. We're in Friendship today. Gotta find out who murdered that woman."

The detectives got into the Ford Explorer and headed south on the East Bank Highway. A not-so-well adorned ribbon of road in close proximity to the murky waters of the Demerara River. The river was born far beyond the cities of

McKenzie and Wismar and into Malali where it began as a freshwater riverlet cascading down a foothill.

By 12:00 noon, they reached their destination. The men fanned out along Friendship's streets. They questioned residents. No one seemed to have seen or heard anything until one resident came forward. The forty-five year old carpenter and father of four told the detectives he accidently injured his leg while working in his yard three days ago. He said he went to a Soesdyke dispenser for medication to treat his wound.

"And what happened after that Mr. Ramdeen?" Martin Brogan asked the man.

"I flagged down a minibus in Soesdyke so I can get back home."

"What color of minibus it was?"

"It was brown."

"Any other passengers on board?"

"Yes."

"Who?"

"An old woman. She was telling the driver she was born in Georgetown but lived in Canada for a long time."

"Were you able to see the number of the vehicle?"

"No. I didn't even think of looking at it."

"When did you hear of this woman's death?"

"I saw it on TV, Officer. And I was shocked when I learned that it happened right in my neighborhood."

"OK, Mr. Ramdeen. You've been a big help. We'll contact you if ever we need you."

"Sure, sir."

Martin Brogan and his partner headed back to Georgetown for the autopsy results of their latest murder victim.

By 3:30 p.m., they were in the clinic of the pathologist. She ushered the men into her office.

"Hello, Doc. How's it going?" Alan Ramsammy asked.

"Good," the woman said forcing an obligatory smile. "The report is out on that body I picked up in Friendship two days ago."

"OK, Doctor DeAbrue. The faster the better. What's her name?" Brogan asked.

"Monica Robinson, a former Guyanese national turned Canadian citizen."

"Interesting," Brogan answered. "What was the cause of death?"

"Two bullet wounds to the face. One bullet exited her forearm when she instinctively brought her hands to her face to deflect the slug. Here are your bullets."

Ramsammy gathered the spent slugs that were in a small plastic bag.

"How long was she dead before we found her, Doc?" Brogan asked.

"Give and take ten or twelve hours."

"OK."

The detectives got into the Explorer and headed to the forensic unit of the police department.

The technician checked the bullets under a microscope. He looked for tiny imperfections from the weapon's barrel imprinted on the slug.

The man's eyes widened in alarm when he called the detectives in the laboratory.

"We got something here, Detective Brogan."

"I'm all ears man. What you've got?"

"Remember that man who was found buried in Le Repentir Cemetery a couple of months ago."

"Yes. I remember."

"The marks on the bullet found in his body match the marks on the bullets found in the skull of Monica Robinson, our latest victim."

"No, shit!" Alan Ramsammy gawked in disbelief. "That same bastard is the one who killed those people. Those bullets are from the same gun."

"That's right," Brogan added. "We'll pick up that report as soon as its finished."

"Sure. First thing in the morning."

There was a brief silence as the men got into the Ford Explorer. Brogan was the first to speak.

"That guy in Friendship said he got into a brown minibus from Soesdyke where he saw the woman from Canada. She ended up dead. And remember the Palm Tree Hotel, a man with a brown minibus stayed on the fourth floor in that room overlooking Caneview Avenue and Greenheart Street. Our man is a minibus driver."

"Sounds right to me."

"Maybe on Monday we'll take a ride to the airport and watch for a brown minibus."

"Who knows. Might be able to spot him."

"If we get lucky."

CHAPTER 12

That evening, Brogan took Nadira Gobin to Avenue of the Republic in Lacytown. She replaced the dead cell phone battery at CellSmart Electronics.

"Do you think that man is going to call me again, Martin?"

"Good question. It's left to be seen."

"I'll get another phone so we both can communicate. Remember Brickdam has my cell bugged. Don't want anyone to listen in on our conversation," Nadira said. "Furthermore if that man ever calls, I don't have to answer my original phone."

"He knows the police is looking for his butt."

"Will he ever be caught, Martin?"

"I'm sure we'll get him. He's bound to slip up one of these days."

"When he's caught and I go back to New York, I don't know if I ever want to go back to my job or live in the same house."

"Why you say that?"

"I can't live in that big house without Cyril."

"What will you do? You've got to live. Besides you'll have bills to pay."

"Sure."

"You told me you worked as a bank teller at Chase Manhattan Bank. Will your wages be enough to pay your bills?"

"Probably not. My husband paid all the bills. He had a good job at the Metropolitan Transit Authority."

"What kind of outfit was that?"

"New York City transit system. Trains, buses and subways. Cyril did maintenance for years."

"Ever thought of putting your house on the market?"

"That will definitely be a possibility. I'll get a smaller place and survive off my late husband's pension, life insurance and social security."

"Who's looking after your house now?"

"My son and his wife."

"Good arrangement."

"Maybe I'll ask you to come to America with me, Martin, when that time comes."

"I'll love to, Nadira," Brogan responded after gasping for an instant in stunned silence.

"Will that be okay with you?"

"I have no problems with that."

"What about your other women?"

"Nothing serious. Just friends."

"No romantic relationships, Martin? I know how women can get. Very tenacious when they see a tall, handsome man like you."

"No one of consequence since my wife walked out on me. Except you."

Nadira did not respond. But her face flushed as she inspired air, hot and voluptuous. Her gaze mingled with fondness and affection.

That Friday evening turned out to be warm and humid with a threat of a heavy thunderstorm. Martin and Nadira went to Windies Sport Bar and Grill on Middle Street. Nadira wore a beautiful dress. The material was a rich, polished fabric Cyril had bought her at Lord and Taylor in New York City. It was not blue or a light shade of purple. But the color was caught somewhere between those two. A delicate indigo, like the horizon just after sunset. And the neckline. Those had grown lower and yet lower as the decades unfolded. But that one barely occluded Nadira's nipples.

They sat at a table far from the bar.

Two minutes later a waitress showed up.

"What can I get you?"

"Two burgers," Nadira answered. "Well done with double cheese and fries."

"Are you ordering for him too?"

"Yes," Nadira answered. "Anything else Martin?"

"Sure. Add five chicken fingers with hot sauce."

"Anything to drink?"

Nadira looked at Brogan as if giving him permission to order her drink.

He did not disappoint her.

"A glass of dry wine for the lady and I'll have a bottle of Banks beer."

They chatted over dinner as the night wore on. Nadira told him how much she was enjoying his company. He praised her for her courage and her ability to move on after the loss of her husband.

"I like being with you too, Nadira," he told her. "I'll be here for you as long as you want me to."

Tears welled up in her eyes as she pondered his words. Brogan reached across the table and dried her eyes with a soft tissue. He held her slender hands.

Slowly what he said registered in her mind. She quickly recovered her composure as her face brightened with a gracious smile.

"You're a wonderful man, Martin. I think I like you."

"Same here, Nadira. You're a pretty woman. I feel the same way too."

They went to the floor and danced. Martin taught her to shoot pool, then they watched a game of rugby on television.

She got close to Brogan. He sensed that she wanted to hold him. To embrace him. And he found it difficult to break the cycle her affirmation had cast over him. He wondered if what was going on was really happening in real life. To fall for a woman took time. Not a weekend or two, he pondered.

But the contrary was happening to him. At that time, he didn't give a brewer's fart that Nadira was Indo-Guyanese. Deep in his mind, his feelings for a woman he didn't know much of, was intensifying.

They left Windies at 1:30 a.m. Brogan drove to his house in Cummings Lodge with Nadira close to him.

When he closed his front door, he turned to face her. She slipped her arms around his neck as another urge had taken control of them. Brogan pulled her body firmly against his. They stood holding and kissing each other. He felt as though he had reached the summit of Mount Roraima.

Then he whispered in her ear.

"I dig you, Nadira. You're a lovely woman."

"I love you too, Martin," she responded to him in a low, soft and sibilant voice. Not yearning for anything more other than that moment. All inhibitions and reservations that lingered in her psyche were quickly swept aside. She tasted his saliva. Ragged with desire and mingled with the beer he downed. He kissed her again and again as her hands snaked across his shoulders and chest. Nadira felt the vigor in those arms that clutched her as she perceived with certainty the culmination of that evening at Windies.

Finally she pulled back and grabbed his hand. She led him through the house and up the stairs towards his bedroom.

CHAPTER 13

That Saturday, Martin and Nadira spent every moment together. She cooked him curried chicken and rice for lunch and later that evening, they visited Club Blue Note and listened to jazz. On Sunday, they had dinner at the Maharaja Palace. They got home at midnight and lay on the couch in each other's arms watching TV far into the night.

Monday morning came without warning. Nadira made breakfast. The two kissed, then Brogan left for police headquarters in Brickdam Road.

He thought of the woman he left lying in his bed. A woman with whom he was romantically involved after knowing her for such a short time. He wondered if she would feel the same about him in time to come as she was doing then. Was the entire process just an orgasmic fling? And one day would Nadira Gobin walk out on him the way Olive did? And as much as they believed they knew each other, they really did not. The thoughts gripped his mind. But deep inside, he knew he was falling in love with the widow of a man whose death he was investigating. That reality did not go easy with him. Brogan had never been so ambivalent about anything in his life. Then he blamed his superego for being too tough on him. Morally, it was not forbidden to seek the affection of a dead man's wife, he mused. Cyril Gobin, unfortunately, was non-existent and spending time with his widow Nadira had convinced

Brogan that he had been missing an important aspect of his life. The more interaction they have together, the better the chance existed for a lasting relationship, he pondered.

He pulled into the parking lot at police headquarters on Brickdam Road.

It was 9:30 a.m. Alan Ramsammy was in the office waiting for him.

"Martin, good morning."

"Good morning to you too."

"Looks like you had a dynamite weekend. I can see it on your face."

"Yes, it was a blast."

"The way to go man."

"How about you? What you did Alan?"

"Went to Parika. We visited Julie's brother."

"Good. Now today a Caribbean Airlines Flight is coming in from New York at 12:00 noon. We will go to Cheddi Jagan International about 11:00 a.m."

"We're looking for a brown minibus. We talked about that in briefing with the lieutenant."

"Yes. Remember we got prints on physical evidence left in the cemetery and Friendship. Those prints told us that the same person committed those murders."

"That's for sure."

"We got to get a print of someone driving a brown minibus."

"Good idea. Let's go."

By 10:30 the detectives arrived at the airport. It was a busy place as expected. Vehicles were filling up the parking lots as fast as they were pulling out. Privately owned vehicles, taxis, and minibuses were everywhere. Inside the terminal, red caps were pulling, lifting and hauling luggage while arriving and departing passenger were closely in tow.

"Where do we start, Martin?"

"The minibus area. We've got to look as if we're here to pick someone up. At the same time we are looking for a brown minibus. Make no arrest. All we need is a registration."

"Well. Let's rock and roll."

"Buy yourself a newspaper, Alan, and pretend like you're reading."

"I know the score."

"Whatever you do, don't blow your cover."

"You can count on me."

By 11:30 a.m., Martin Brogan had already looked through the Daily Chronicle from front to back. He stood up, placed the newspaper under his arm. He was about to put the empty Pepsi can in the trash when his phone rang.

"Hello, Martin."

"Yes, Alan. What's up?"

"There's a guy coming in your direction. He's Indo-Guyanese, in his fifties, well built. He's wearing a Hawaiian shirt and dungaree pants."

"Is he driving a brown minibus?"

"Yes, I saw him got out the driver's seat in the parking area. Looks like he's looking for passengers coming off the plane."

"Good job, Alan. He's bound to pass me from where I'm sitting to get in the vicinity of the Caribbean Airlines terminal."

"Fine. I'll stay far behind and meet you at the terminal."

"What he looks like, Alan?"

"He's about six-feet, unshaven with a mean-looking face and salt and pepper hair."

"OK, I'll keep my eyes peeled."

Within minutes Brogan saw a man fitting the description Alan had given him. He was coming up a walkway with a group of other people. Brogan swallowed dryly as he was prepared to expect the unexpected. Never confront a suspect without hard evidence. It could avoid a firefight and eventually save his life. That was a creed he never abandoned when he walked the streets of Georgetown as a constable and supervised others as a sergeant. The absence of that belief caused his father's demise when he was a constable years ago on Saffon Street. The difference between life and death was entirely unmistakable. When he saw his father with a gunshot wound to the abdomen at the Georgetown Hospital, Brogan knew that his father was gone. In his place was a cadaverous and frigid reflection of who he had been. As a boy, Brogan felt like a deflated balloon. He slumped in his mother's arms and began to sob. A year and one half later, his mother died from depression and a disease that ravaged her kidneys.

Martin Brogan regarded the man with an inward sneer as he observed him sitting by a soda fountain. For a fleeting moment, outrage and bitterness clouded his mind. But as a lawman, a miraculous wave washed away those thoughts. Profiling was unacceptable. A man was innocent until proven guilty. The man whipped out a pack of cigarettes and placed one between his lips. He struck a match, lit the cigarette and ordered a can of Pepsi.

About ten minutes later the man finished his cigarette and soda. He flipped the cigarette butt on the walkway and trashed the can. He looked at his watch. Quickly he uprighted his pear-shaped body and headed further into the terminal.

Martin Brogan and his partner sprung into action. They retrieved the cigarette butt and the empty soda can with gloved hands and quickly left the area.

Chapter 14

Two days later, results of the physical evidence that the detectives had gathered at the airport were discussed at a briefing on Brickdam Road.

Brogan and Ramsammy sat in a conference room with a few uniformed ranks. A man named Edgar Kilkenny, a police captain in his late fifties, was the officer in charge. He had come to Georgetown from McKenzie City back in 1968. Quickly he made rank for his quick thinking and brutality. In his younger days, the man could have been characterized as a distinguished beast of prey. Wide nose, horse mouth, thick brows and a Neanderthal jaw. His contemptuous eyes and a repulsive face caused would-be criminals to turn on their heels.

"The evidence that detectives Brogan and Ramsammy have collected at Cheddi Jagar International Airport have been analyzed. And men, guess what? They matched evidence we've collected at the scenes of the other murders. The registration of the brown minibus leads back to a man whose name is Mohan Basdeo. He lives at 707 Plumrose Avenue in Better Hope."

"What's the next move, Captain?" a young uniformed rank asked with eagerness. "Is it not time to make an arrest? We've got the evidence."

"The detective will fill you in on that. Detective Brogan, you've got it from here," Kilkenny said and exited the room with a portly waddle.

Martin Brogan took the lectern. He told the ranks that a warrant would be obtained to search Mohan Basdeo's residence to further implicate him in the murders.

"When will we get a search warrant?" another rank asked.

"It's in the making. We have already submitted information to a magistrate in the jurisdiction involved showing probable cause. Fingerprints that we gathered from physical evidence at the crime scenes are deemed as probable cause. They have put Mr. Basdeo at the scenes of the murders. The magistrate will review the evidence and approve our request for a warrant."

"It won't be too long before he's behind bars," another rank was able to say.

"Correct," Brogan answered. "But we have to be damn certain that 707 Plumrose Avenue is the man's place of abode. Anything else on that Detective Ramsammy?"

"Yes, Detective. A police cruiser drove by the place earlier today. The residence is a small ranch style house painted white. To its left is a two-storied brick dwelling with a soft yellow color. On the right is a low, unpainted frame bungalow. Across Plumrose Avenue, facing the suspect's house, is a grocery store. The name is Lallman's Foods. We can't miss the suspect's home."

"Anyone has a question?" Brogan asked.

There was no response.

"Now it behooves everyone to be safe. You all know that Mr. Basdeo was deported from the United States twelve years ago. He did five years in a federal prison for attempting to smuggle narcotics through a New York airport. The man is not new to crime. He's a hardened felon who is armed and dangerous. If he confronts you with a weapon, shoot to kill."

"I don't have a problem with that, Detective Brogan," one uniformed rank said as an improvised smile flashed across his face.

"Once the search warrant is in place, we'll move in on him tonight at 10:00 p.m."

That night at 9:15 p.m., Martin Brogan, Alan Ramsammy and six uniformed ranks took to the Liliendaal Expressway.

Their destination was Better Hope. They were armed with a search warrant for a house situated at 707 Plumrose Avenue in Better Hope. It's occupant, a man known as Mohan Basdeo, was to be brought to police headquarters in Georgetown. He was to be questioned as a person of interest in the murders of three persons.

Forty minutes later, the Ford Explorer occupied by Brogan and Ramsammy with two police cruisers behind turned off the highway. The vehicles moved slowly on Plumrose Avenue until they came to 707. There was no brown minibus in the driveway. Brogan winced in surprise as he got on the police radio.

"Sergeant MacDonald, looks like we're in for a shocker. The vehicle is not here. We will go in anyway and execute our search warrant."

"I copy you, Detective Brogan. We are ready."

The lawmen spilled out across the bridge and towards the front door. One rank was armed with a battering ram.

"Police! Police! Open the door! Search warrant!" one rank shouted as he banged on the door.

Quickly another cop ran to the back yard and stood by the door. His Colt Mustang .380 automatic drawn and ready. His eyes sweeping the landscape for movements. Meanwhile in the front yard Brogan's weapon, a Browning high-powered 9-mm Parabellum was out of its holster and was at the ready.

All other ranks drew their weapons and were at the ready. Their voices strained in unison.

"The door will come down! Open up!" Like helmeted warriors, swords drawn high, ready to finish a vanquished foe.

Suddenly the door was opening. Before them stood an Indo-Guyanese woman in her mid-forties. She regarded the lawmen with saucerlike eyes. Her freckled face ablaze. She had thinning black hair and wore a burlap, shapeless blue dress. She had narrow cringing shoulders like she was ducking a thrown object.

"What on earth did I do!" the woman shouted savagely, with a start of surprise.

"Is Mohan at home? Where is he?" one cop shouted with a sardonic voice.

"He went to the shop to get cigarettes!" the woman answered irately.

"We have a warrant to search this place. Who are you, ma'am?"

"I'm Stella Tawari, Mohan's girlfriend."

By then, the cops were going through the house. Mohan Basdeo was nowhere to be found.

The cops found a room with suitcases packed with men's and women's clothes, jewelry, cell phones and U.S. currency.

"Did Mohan tell you where he got all this merchandise?"

"He said he bought them from a man at the airport."

"Miss Tawari, when was the last time you talked to Mohan?"

"A few minutes ago. I called him when I saw the police cars outside. I thought people were coming to hurt or rob me."

"OK. You'll have to come to Georgetown with us."

"No. No. I don't want to go to prison. I didn't do anything!" the woman responded, spewing out her words with anger and revulsion.

"Turn around, Miss Tawari. Place your hands behind your back now!" the cop demanded gruffly.

They slapped the woman with handcuffs. She and boxes of evidence were transported to police headquarters.

A perimeter of yellow police tape was placed around the residence. It was deemed a crime scene. Martin Brogan radioed police headquarters.

"Captain Glascow, this is Detective Brogan. We executed the search warrant. It must have been the suspect's lucky day. His girlfriend said he was out buying cigarettes when we entered the residence. She called him with her cell phone when she saw us on Plumrose Avenue. That spooked him. Now we have an active manhunt. Mohan Basdeo is on the run."

"Let him run as far as he can, Brogan. But remember he can't hide. We'll get that sucker."

"That right, Captain."

"I'll set up a couple of ranks to watch the house for a couple of days. You and your men can call it a night. We'll start again in the morning."

"Good idea Captain Glascow."

It was 12:30 a.m. when Stella Tawari was fingerprinted and placed in a holding cell at police headquarters. All evidence retrieved from the house was checked, labeled and stored in an evidence room at police headquarters.

By 8:00 a.m. the following morning, Stella Tawari was led from her cell to an interrogation room. Two detectives, a male and female, sat across the table from her.

"This conversation is being recorded, Miss Tawari, and can be held against you in a court of law," the female detective said.

"Who cares," the prisoner responded.

"You have the right to remain silent or to request an attorney if you need one."

"Detective, I'm not in any trouble."

"Are you willing to tell us what you know of Mohan Basdeo and how he was found to be in possession of all that money and merchandise found in the house you both share?"

"I don't know anything."

"How long were you living with Mr. Basdeo?"

"About five years."

"So you ought to have known that those items were in the house."

"He told me not to go in that room. Furthermore he always kept it locked."

"Stella, Mr. Basdeo is suspected of killing at least three people he picked up with his minibus at the airport," the male detective said.

"No. I don't believe that."

"Believe what you want Stella. One thing you've gotta know. When Basdeo goes down, he'll take you along with him," the male detective answered.

"Meaning what?"

"If the crown prosecutor gets a death penalty conviction against your boyfriend, you will be put to death too as a conspirator."

"No. No. That's not fair!" Stella Tawari screamed as she stared at her interrogators with fascinated horror. "I did not kill anyone."

"Who did?" the female detective asked.

"Oh God. Now I'll die. Mohan said he'll kill me if I ever tell anyone. And Heaven knows, I don't want to die!" the woman hollered and wept as she regarded the detectives with a catatonic stare. One interrogator handed the woman a glass of water and some tissues.

The male interrogator gave Stella Tawari a long searching look before he spoke.

"We want the truth, Miss Tawari. We know it wasn't you who killed three people. But somehow Mr. Basdeo must have told you something relating to the murders. Your knowledge of that makes you an accessory to a felony. In other words, you're a co-conspirator."

"No. No, I don't even know the people he killed! Mohan told me he hated Guyanese people coming back to spend time in this country because he was deported over twelve years ago."

"Is that so?"

"Yes. He said he loved to kill them and take their belongings."

"Why didn't you leave that house and notify the police?"

"Officer. Are you crazy? Mohan threatened my life many times. He told me that if I ever tell the police, I'll be the next on his list."

"Will you be willing to testify against him if the crown prosecutor cuts you a deal?"

"What kinda deal?"

"You won't go to prison."

"Sound good. But I can never ever go back to Better Hope. He'll come and get me. Besides, that's his house."

"You will be protected in a witness protection program."

CHAPTER 15

It was about 2:30 p.m. two days later. An all points bulletin was issued across the country for Mohan Basdeo, a brawny man in his fifties, six-feet-one inch tall with a fleshy face, high cheekbones and grizzled, graying hair. The TV newscaster said the man was suspected in the murders of three people coming to Georgetown from overseas. He was armed and dangerous with a ruthless, deceitful and sociopathic personality. The report stated that Basdeo should not be approached if seen by anyone. But the police should be notified immediately.

In the town of Felicity, not far from Better Hope, a telephone was ringing off its hook on Peach Street.

A man named Joseph Pollard lying in bed with a gangling palsied body, reached for the phone with clawlike fingers.

"Hello. Who is this?" he asked in a caustic voice.

"Joseph. This is Mohan, your friend."

"Man, why are you calling me?"

"Joe, we got trouble!"

"No! Watch what you're talkin'. Not we man! It's you. You're the son-of-a-bitch in trouble."

"The police are after my ass."

"Mohan, that's a foregone conclusion. I told you to be careful. Didn't I?"

"It's Stella, Joe. She told the cops every damn thing."

"Mohan, I saw it on the news. They hauled away all your shit to Brickdam. Stella went so far as to cut a deal with the prosecutor."

"What that means?"

"It's easy man. She'll walk after testifying against you. Your butt is going to the gallows. That woman judge doesn't play."

"Shit! That stupid slut, Stella! I should have put her goofy ass down a long time ago."

"I told you before about that crazy bitch. Now you're screwed. It's too late now!"

"What do I do now, Joe? I can't even walk the streets of Better Hope. The friggin' cops are swarming all over the place. Can't come home no more."

"Where are you now, Mohan?"

"In Berbice. The west coast, Litchfield."

"That's way across the Abary River, man. You better keep your ass in hiding. If they find you, that will be some serious shit. Whatever you do, Mohan, don't call my goddamn name!"

"Why should I do that? I call this crap on myself. I'm the friggin' duffer here!"

"You can say that again."

"Hey, Joe, I think I gotta go now. I'm using a public phone on the roadside and I'm running out of change. Couldn't use my cell. I know the cops already have it bugged."

"Good idea, Mohan."

"I think I'll go in the interior and shack with the Amerindians. They'll never catch my ass."

"Go for it, you schmuck! But get this, don't ever call me. I'll call you."

Mohan Basdeo hung up the public phone and walked over to the minibus. He got in the driver's seat as his eyes searched the landscape. His face bearing a somber expression.

It was three days since he left Better Hope, he deliberated. Just because the cops got wind of his hustle. And every time he took a nap in the confines of his minibus, he was in the old neighborhood again. And whom one would imagine he always saw. Stella Tawari. She was standing by the stove, cooking his favorite meal. Her dimpled, alcohol-roughened face, gave way to mirthful crinkles about her eyes. His dream was comforting while it lasted. But after he awoke, he grumbled with rage as his vociferous thoughts for Stella continued.

He started the vehicle without knowing where he was headed. That Litchfield was almost an entirely Afro-Guyanese neighborhood trespassed on his mind. He thought of the color of his skin. It was dark. But that was where the similarity began and ended. He would stand out like a sore thumb in Litchfield or neighboring Belladrum. Thus increasing his chance of being busted by the police.

Mohan Basdeo started driving due east for the next ninety minutes until he reached Rosignol. It was a small town, nestled on the west bank of the Berbice River. To Basdeo, the place that he had journeyed to was necessary. It had a port, the Rosignol Stelling. A main point of getting to the city of New Amsterdam on the east bank, if and when it became necessary.

He cruised the streets for half hour, looking forward to a melancholy evening to suit his mood. But a sun setting in the west was bright and cool. It smacked him full in the face as his thoughts gyrated in nauseating spirals.

Then he saw a woman flagging down his minibus. Her hair long and lustrous in a subdued style. Her gentle footsteps slightly echoed across the pavement.

Basdeo pulled the minibus to a stop. The woman articulated in a low murmur.

"Hollywood Bar, please."

"Hop in. I'm not familiar with the area. You've got to tell me where it is. I'm new in town."

"It's in Blairmont. I'll tell you how to get there," the woman said as she got into a seat in the passenger's compartment. She carried a slinky body. Her mouth appeared mint-fresh and her nails, from fingers to toes, were well cared for.

"Hollywood Bar must be a fun place."

"Yes. It sure is. I'm a dancer there."

"I know you must be good."

"So the patrons say."

"I'll like to come there sometime."

"Anytime you want. You'll see me in motion."

Twenty minutes later, the minibus pulled up on Lancaster Street and came to a stop in front of the Hollywood Bar.

"How much is the fare, lover boy?"

"What do you normally pay?"

"Fifty dollars."

"I'll take the fifty."

The woman gave Basdeo a fifty dollar bill and got out of the minibus.

"Are you coming in, honey?" the woman asked as she regarded him provocatively.

"You go. I'll come in after I park the vehicle."

The woman nodded and walked to the entrance with a voluptuous sway. The sound of music was heard, mingled with great gusts of nasty laughter. Cars lined the roadside due to an overcrowded parking lot.

Basdeo smoked a cigarette as he shot flitting glances to and from the door. He thought of what had just transpired. The woman, he figured, possessed an unmistakable air of natural intimacy. Unlike Stella Tawari, that ragdoll. She was young, lustful and pretty. But her artificial world could one day come crashing down in a landscape where purveyors of the streets lived and thrived with impunity. His life, he meditated, was closely parallel to hers. There was a time when he rolled downhill like a snowball and not thinking of the consequences. But the time had come for him to take an inventory of his life. His tumultuous past hung before his eyes like mist in a valley. He murdered people for their possessions. And shared his spoils with others who claimed to be his friends. Those so-called friends had been avoiding him like the plague. Where were they at that time? But Basdeo knew the deal. They were in hiding in an effort to save their own asses. And at the same time, they threw him to the dogs. Was it too late for him to restructure his life?

But in Basdeo's mind, he would not allow himself to be eaten by the dogs in Brickdam Road without a fight. If ever he went down, he intended to drag Joe Pollard and all the other jitterbugs with him.

He parked the minibus at the roadside and entered the Hollywood Bar. It was six thirty in the evening and the place was already crowded. People were consuming beer, wine and whiskey like they were going out of style. A topless female dancer with almost nothing for an underwear revolved around a mahogany pole. Her movements wanton, lewd and voluptuous. Spectators' eyes glinted with pleasure. Basdeo took a seat close to the dancer. He recognized her as the same young woman who had ridden in his minibus. Groups of men, young and old, were juxtapositioned to the dancer. Like foxes by a chicken coop. Men of diverse background and careers. They stuffed money in her thong and tried to touch her. Then the dancer saw Basdeo. She flashed him a dirty little grin and advanced towards him with a pertly wiggle.

CHAPTER 16

That morning at police headquarters in Brickdam Road, the warmth inside the briefing room felt heavy, like a steamed towel against his body. Martin Brogan and other ranks listened to Edgar Kilkenny, the captain in charge of operations during his briefing.

"It has been two weeks since the suspect, Mohan Basdeo, was able to slip through our dragnet in Better Hope," the man said as his long-jawed face and piercing eyes held the group with an austere look. "The major told me yesterday that his boss, the assistant superintendent, had been getting on his nerve, because the public is scared as hell of this guy being on the loose. I say to all you ranks and I mean it. Shit only rolls downhill. Not up. If the pressure comes down on me, I'll pass that crap down the line. You gotta get out there and make an arrest. I don't give a shit. Just get this son-of-a-bitch off the streets. The suck stops here!"

The man took a sip from a glass of water sitting on his desk. He looked at the ranks, fixing each person with a stubborn stare.

"Any questions!" he fumed.

No one responded.

"Get outa' here, guys. If you want to maintain your career as cops, it behooves you all to find that bastard," Edgar Kilkenny ended in a brisk, businesslike voice.

The cops filed out of the briefing room and headed to their assignments.

Brogan and Ramsammy walked towards the Ford Explorer. That day they were headed to the town of Enmore to check out a telephone tip of a brown minibus seen in the neighborhood.

Ramsammy got into the driver's seat.

"Looks like ole man Kilkenny is fired up today, Martin."

"Yes. That cat is always blowing off some steam."

"He said Maxwell Graham, the assistant superintendent of police, is putting his feet to the fire."

"You know how that started. Don't you?"

"No," Ramsammy said.

"A business woman on Homestretch Avenue called the mayor's office and said a man in a brown minibus was tailgating her from her job one day."

"So. What happened?"

"We all know the mayor of Georgetown and the Commissioner of Police are buddies. He made a call to the comish and the rest you know, Alan."

"Politics man, never a dull moment."

"That's correct. We better be going. Enmore is about fifteen miles from here."

"Sure. How is your lady friend, Martin?"

"She's doin' good. She moved into my place a week ago. Didn't I tell you?"

"You sure didn't."

"Yes, fella. I'm living the life. Lots of loving."

"Good."

After twenty-five minutes of driving, the detectives reached Enmore, a place roughly two square miles with a population of about three thousand residents.

The detectives pulled the Ford Explorer off Railway Embankment Highway to Station Road. Police headquarters was tucked under the shadow of a giant tamarind tree on Station Road. An unadorned one-storied structure with a dilapidated mahogany desk and a few metal chairs. The front windows were smeared with streaks of paint. Through them in the distance, one could faintly see first the main drag, then a more or less littered farmyard running across a wide spread. Beyond those were the turbulent waters of the Atlantic Ocean.

A picture decorated the wall of a brightly colored and crude toucan with abstract designs around it.

Behind the desk sat a thin wiry man. He introduced himself as Sergeant Harry Sahoy. A man about forty-seven with a heavy black mustache, tobacco-chewing and huge exophthalmic eyes.

"It's nice to meet you, Sergeant Sahoy," Martin Brogan said after introducing himself and his partner.

"OK. Let's get moving," Sergeant Sahoy said as he motioned to the detectives to grab their chairs. "Based on the APB and talk about Mohan Basdeo in the news, a man in town called us a few days ago and said he saw a person driving a brown minibus fitting the description of our suspect."

"That's the reason we're here, Sergeant," Brogan quipped.

"We'll talk to the man who called our station."

"Ready when you are."

The three men left the station.

Brogan and Ramsammy followed the police sergeant in the Ford Explorer. The vehicles turned off the East Coast Highway and traveled south along a dismal, blighted ribbon of road called Charles Sumra Trail. Houses lay scattered on both sides of the road. Heavy rains of the previous day and night had abated, leaving the atmosphere shrouded in a thick, sultry and misty web.

Within twelve minutes they located their destination. A rambling, old English-style cottage, once a magnificent fixture during colonial times. That day, it was no more than a crumbling structure in darkened and profound disarray.

A Toyota Landcruiser sat in the driveway surrounded by half a dozen dilapidated and evil-looking junk cars.

The cops got out of their vehicles. Sergeant Sahoy led the way. At the door, he reached out a hand and drummed on the hardwood. Moments passed as the men awaited a response. Then a sound was heard. Like someone unlocking a giant bolt. Then the huge, cumbersome greenheart door swung inward and opened. Moaning and groaning on rusted out and unoiled hinges.

A pot-bellied, aging man stood in the doorway. He held the cops with an impatient stare.

"Mr. Sugrim. I'm Sergeant Sahoy from the police station."

"Yes. I know you. You were here before."

"That's right. These men with me are detectives from Georgetown. Detectives Brogan and Ramsammy."

"Holy cow! Am I in trouble?"

"No, you're not. It's about the call you made to me about seeing a brown minibus in the neighborhood a couple of days ago."

"That vehicle. The minibus."

"Yes, Mr. Sugrim, that same minibus," Brogan answered, joining in.

"Maybe you can talk to my neighbor across the street. That brown minibus dropped him at his house that day. I wasn't able to get the number on the plates."

"Are you sure of that, Mr. Sugrim?" Ramsammy asked after a long silence.

"As sure as the sun rises. I've got no reason to be untruthful young man," Sugrim said as a flicker of discomfort passed over his face.

"OK, sir," Ramsammy answered.

The lawmen spilled across Charles Sumra Trail and walked towards a low cement house along a grassy path. No one spoke as Detective Brogan knocked on the door. A man in his late forties, standing nearly six feet, stood before the detectives and uniformed rank. He was a thin man but brawny with clean denim overalls. His salt and pepper hair was neatly trimmed. He moved his eyes slowly from one lawman to the other. His deep-set, Caucasian eyes appearing black and flat. And without moisture.

His face grew chalky with a sudden fear but it quickly normalized after becoming aware that he alone was conscious of that fear.

Brogan smiled vaguely at the man. "Good afternoon," he said pleasantly. The man did not respond but looked at each lawman's face owlishly. After a brief moment he answered.

"Good afternoon, Officers. Is there a problem?"

"No. Not really. I am Detective Brogan and my partner here is Alan Ramsammy."

"Don't bother to introduce Sergeant Sahoy. I know him in Plantation Enmore for years," the man said. "What seems to be the problem?"

"A brown minibus brought you home a few days ago, sir. Do you remember?" Brogan asked the man.

"My name is Jairam, Detective Brogan. I live here with my wife and children. What was your question again?"

Martin Brogan repeated his question.

"That day I drove to Clonbrook Village to my job at the hardware store. But while coming back, my car broke down. After ten minutes, a brown minibus pulled up. The driver offered to bring me home for a hundred dollars."

"Were there any other passengers in the vehicle?"

"Two black men."

"Did they say where they were going?"

"Yes. One said he was going to Litchfield and the other fellow said he lived in Fort Wellington."

"Was the bus driver talking a lot?"

"Yes. He was mouthing off."

"About what?"

"He said he wanted to sell his minibus and asked if we knew anyone who wanted to buy his bus."

"What was your answer?"

"I told him that I didn't know of anyone who will buy a bus in these hard times."

"How did he respond to that?"

"That man was angry about something, Detective Brogan. He was yelling obscenities at the police. He said once he gets to Rosignol, he intends to leave the country, because the police commissioner and politicians were no good anymore."

Later that evening, Martin Brogan and Alan Ramsammy headed back to police headquarters in Georgetown.

"Our man appears to be very elusive," Ramsammy said, muttering peevishly under his breath.

"We'll get him, Alan. The longest road has an end."

"I know that for sure. I got this feeling that he left the Georgetown area a long time ago."

"The man could be anywhere."

"Yes, especially in a place where he can use that minibus to make himself some money."

"True. Right now I know he's broke to the world. The police confiscated all that money and jewelry he stole from people so he's got to be running on empty."

"He's hurting real bad. That I know for sure."

"I don't suppose he's got any relative around."

"No, both parents are deceased and he's the only child."

"He's the only hell his parents ever raised," Brogan said as his face broke into an ironic smile.

CHAPTER 17

The piercing sound of a police siren, far in the night, gave him a rude awakening. He shot upright in bed as the sound got closer. Tires hissed on the asphalt.

Was it rain? A vague thought flashed across his mind as he was still groggy from sleep. Were those cops hot on his trail? The thought shrank his lungs as if siphoned empty. And suddenly, he felt as if unable to breathe.

Fear encroached on his brain.

Then he began to list his surroundings in pieces. The bulky shadow of the vanity besides his bed, the strangled drone of the air conditioner through the wall and the penetrating noise of the siren as it drew closer and yet closer.

Quickly he sprung from his bed in the semi-dark room and lurked towards the window overlooking the street below. He gaped in stunned silence as his trembling hands parted the shade. His eyes fixed on the street with a scorching stare.

A police cruiser had stopped a speeding car in front of the Church View International Hotel where he was staying.

He saw the cop got from his car and walked to the Nissan with an antagonistic gait. He said a few words to the driver and wrote him a summon. It was 4:30 a.m. in the town of New Amsterdam. A city located four miles up the Berbice River from the Atlantic Ocean.

Mohan Basdeo's face brightened when he saw the cop made a right turn in the direction of Smithfield Township.

The driver of the Nissan started his engine and headed north towards East Canje.

He figured that situation was too close for comfort. He never wanted to be near cops. His sustained, rancorous feelings for them caused his hands to ball up in fists of fury. Deep in his thoughts he reasoned that the Church View International Hotel and New Street were not the place he wanted to be.

He loved the Hollywood Bar in Blairmont. There was where he met a rich rice farmer from Ithaca, who bought his minibus. Basdeo told the man he sold insurance for the Hand in Hand Mutual Insurance Company in Georgetown, while he hired a driver to work the minibus.

"That cocksucker didn't work out," he told the man one day over a table full of whiskey.

"Why?" the man asked with a look of surprise on his face.

"Instead of working, the fellow ran after women and pocketed most of the money he made driving my bus."

"That's bad."

"So I yanked my bus from that swindler."

"You did the right thing. Are you willing to sell it? Looks like a good vehicle."

"Sure I'll sell it. I want to go back selling insurance. It's an easy job."

"Not in Blairmont. People don't buy insurance."

"I know. That's why I gotta get back to Georgetown."

"What brought you all the way here in the first place?"

"Put an ad in the Sunday Chronicle to sell the minibus."

"Got any hits?"

"Yes. This fellow living in this town answered the ad and told me he wanted to buy the bus."

"What happened?"

"He never showed up at the Hollywood Bar where we arranged to meet. It's now been four days."

"Man's a phony. I know his kind."

"That's right. Four days and I haven't seen this joker."

"Man, he's friggin' with you."

"It seems so."

"I'll buy the bus from you. How much you are asking?"

"It's three years old and pretty much brand new. Are you willing to shell out eight hundred thousand? Only has thirty thousand miles."

"I'll get my mechanic to look it over. If everything goes well, we've got a deal."

And so it was.

A week ago Basdeo sold the minibus to a man named Frederick Ragnauth. A rice farmer and money man from the west bank of the Berbice River. Then he caught a taxi out of Blairmont and journeyed to New Amsterdam.

Quickly Mohan Basdeo came back to reality when he thought of his suitcase stuffed with money and a .38 caliber revolver under his pillow.

He had it all, he figured. Money and a gun. When he was sent back to Guyana, he remembered, he was broke. He found odd jobs around Georgetown. From grocery store salesman to street sweeper. Then he landed a job as a bus driver from Hadfield Street in Lacytown to Peter's Hall on the East Bank of Demerara.

Basdeo made money for the man who hired him. He was honest and showed conscientiousness. After a few years, he bought his own minibus and started working the streets of Georgetown. Things were good at first until one evening, a lone passenger put a gun to his head on Middle Road in West La Penitence and demanded money. Basdeo complied and gave up his day's earnings. That event infuriated him. He purchased a gun on the streets of Tiger Bay for his own protection the next day. It was the Model 38 also known as the Bodyguard Airweight with a 2-inch barrel. It was Mohan Basdeo's only real friend.

He lay back in bed, huddling in the semi-dark room. His heart clenching, as he wondered if he'd made the right decision in crossing the Berbice River. But he figured he had gone too far to back out then. For him, it was a situation that was beyond his control. He knew that he was a man on the run. All it behooved him to do was to avoid the police and lay low as possible. Because he'd be sitting pretty for a hell of a long time.

At 8:00 a.m. that morning, he still wrestled with uncertainty as to his safety at the hotel. He came down the stairs from the third floor with suitcase in hand and his concealed weapon stuffed between his belt. His bloodhound facial expression was unchanged. Haggard and annoyed. Fitting for a man, metamorphosed from clay to granite.

He sat in the dining room overlooking New Street. A slight morning breeze blowing from east to west, trespassed on his face. A yellow breasted bird blared a note from the boughs of a cashew tree. He ignored the cries while his eyes scoped his surroundings with malicious impudence.

"What's for breakfast this morning, sir?" a low voice yanked him from his ponder. He spun his head around and saw a medium built woman standing by his table with an order pad. To him, she was in her mid-thirties, slender and handsome with large brown eyes and jet black shoulder length hair. Thoughts of his ex-wife in New York City came back to him as if it were yesterday.

"Do you know what you are having?" the woman asked with a quiet Berbician drawl.

"Just thinking," the man said, maintaining her stare as he put down the menu he got from the table. "Bake with salted fish with scrambled eggs and coffee."

"How do you want your eggs?"

"Well done."

"That's all?"

"Yes ma'am."

From his vantage point, Mohan Basdeo watched the woman saunter across the floor. Slants of morning sunlight glowed ahead of her. To him she appeared like an angel. The kind he always wanted to be his woman. The thought cast a sunny feeling in his soul as a growing arousal cascaded through his anatomy. Then he quickly realized that those thoughts were indeed fragments of his imagination. Those days had come and were then gone. His reality was more dramatic. He was a man who had a home one day and the next day it was gone. He was on a serious retreat.

Two days later, Basdeo caught a taxi and headed north to a tiny river town called Corriverton, overlooking Suriname. He checked into a hotel called The Mahogany situated on the highway that led to the towns of Skeldon and Crabwood Creek.

CHAPTER 18

That morning in Georgetown, Detectives Martin Brogan and Alan Ramsammy sat in a conference room with other ranks during a briefing with Edgar Kilkenny, the operations captain in Brickdam.

Brogan and his partner had traversed streets from Better Hope to Enmore in their continuing search for Mohan Basdeo. They chased other leads, culled from the suspect's high school friends, his live-in girlfriend Stella Tawari and an alcoholic street bum who washed Basdeo's minibus at the Hadfield Street taxi park in Georgetown.

When all efforts did not produce any result, Kilkenny's voice was acidic and to the point. "We got a report this morning that a man named Frederick Ragnauth is attempting to register a brown minibus at the department of motor vehicles in New Amsterdam. Now what on earth does that tell us?"

"Basdeo sold the minibus," a uniformed rank answered.

"You're bloody right, constable! The man sold the minibus somewhere in the town of Blairmont. And the vehicle identification number matches the minibus Basdeo owned."

"That's good news," Brogan said.

"Better believe it, Brogan," Kilkenny said. "This time we've got that sucker by the balls!"

"What's our next move, Captain?" Ramsammy asked.

"You know the next move, Ramsammy!" Kilkenny responded, his voice growing frenzied. "You and Brogan are going to Blairmont now, to bring that friggin' crackpot back to Brickdam, even if you've got to hog-tie his nasty punk ass! You turkeys got any questions?"

"No, sir," Ramsammy answered.

"You fellas, got to hell outa here!"

Brogan, Ramsammy and the others walked out the conference room. The detectives climbed into the Ford Explorer, Ramsammy behind the wheel. It was nine thirty on a Tuesday morning. Georgetown was already warm with an unrelenting sun bearing down from a cloudless sky.

Ramsammy started the engine and spoke as he adjusted the rear and side view mirrors.

"Guess the captain is fired up today."

"He's always blowing his top when I see him."

"Maybe his wife isn't giving it up."

"I wouldn't go that far, man. That's his problem."

"That's probably right, Martin. But it isn't that we aren't working our asses off to find this creep."

"True. All the stuff we've been doing the past couple of weeks had to be done."

"Couldn't be avoided if we want to bring closure to this investigation."

"Sure, Alan."

The detectives were both referring to the long, wearisome, fruitless days they had spent interviewing and reinterviewing residents from Better Hope to the town of Enmore on the east coast of Demerara in their effort to locate Mohan

Basdeo. They had run into a brick wall. All the leads they obtained from confidential informers, telephone tips from the public and the news media never panned out. It caused the sleuths to journey on a road that led to nowhere. That day, according to the boss man, Captain Edgar Kilkenny, they were back to square one.

The Explorer traveled east on Brickdam Road then hugged a left on Vlissengen. Quickly it got to Seawall Road.

Ramsammy was the first to speak after the vehicle got on the East Coast Highway.

"Quite a stretch to Blairmont. Sixty miles."

"Sure. How is your gas?"

"Three quarters of a tank."

"That's good."

"I wonder where that moron will be in Blairmont."

"He's got some money on him now. He's got to be in hiding somewhere."

"Blairmont police said he hangs out at the Hollywood Bar on Lancaster Street. He loves to watch a dancer there named Eva Bhagwan doing her thing."

"One of those kinky guys, right?"

"I can't bet on that. Maybe he likes to be in the company of sexy broads."

"I like their company too, but I wouldn't do the things that weirdo has done."

"Hell, no. For you and I, the stakes are too high."

By 12:00 noon, the Ford Explorer pulled into the town of Blairmont and made a right turn on Lancaster

Street. Within minutes, the vehicle pulled in front of the Hollywood Bar.

The place was housed in a one-storied cement building in one of four settlements on the West Berbice Coast. The front of the building overlooked the gloomy waters of the Berbice River and the industrialized section of the Blairmont sugar cane factory.

Ramsammy pulled into a parking spot that had just become vacant.

The detectives walked along a concrete footpath and entered the establishment. The smell of food and liquor was heavy in the air. About a dozen patrons were scattered across the seating area. Men and women. Eating, drinking, talking and laughing. About half a dozen men sat at the bar as an old electric Westinghouse fan convulsed in the ceiling. A jukebox blared a song by Madonna.

Brogan went over to the counter where a man in his early forties with a beefy face, a beer keg belly and a tight-boned gait served liquor.

"Good afternoon, sir," Brogan said.

"Good afternoon," the man replied as he eyed the detectives with an uneasy puzzlement.

"My name's Martin Brogan. This is my partner Alan Ramsammy," Brogan said as he and his partner showed the bartender their credentials.

"What can I do to help you?" the bartender asked as a troubled look dominated his face.

"We're looking for this man. His name's Mohan Basdeo," Ramsammy said as he slid a picture across the counter.

The bartender looked at the picture as he held it between his fingers. Then a grin that feigned friendliness lit up his expression.

"I know this man. He comes here sometimes. But that's not his name. I don't know him as Mohan Basdeo."

"What name do you know him as?" Brogan asked.

"I know him as Walter Chattersingh."

"When last did you see him?"

"Three weeks ago he was here. I think he sold a minibus to Mr. Ragnauth. Afterwards no one has seen him."

"Where Mr. Ragnauth lives?"

"Frederick Ragnauth lives about four miles from here, in Ithaca."

"What's his address?" Ramsammy asked.

"It's a big white house off the highway. The largest house in Ithaca."

"Then we can't miss it."

"Right, Officer. That's true."

"Here's my card," Brogan said to the man. "If you ever see him again, give me a call."

"Sure, detective."

The men left the Hollywood Bar and sped off in the Explorer.

"Our man is using a fake name now, Alan."

"Yes. He thinks he's slick but sooner or later we'll catch up to his hustle."

"Eventually. That time isn't too far off the horizon."

For twenty minutes the vehicle moved south along a winding narrow and unpaved road. Flanked by gentle immortelle and sandbox trees with thick shrubberies blanketing their undergrowth. Locals moved on foot. Their faces twisted in fatigue, or more or less painful physical exertion. Others rode bicycles or mule drawn carts in their never-ending odyssey to survive in an environment where jobs were scarce.

Not too far away, off to the right, an enormous frame building loomed. It was nestled among the vegetation like a sapphire thrown into a field of coastal Bermuda grass. The detectives saw that the house was a gigantic bungalow half a mile from the highway. The manicured lawn, extending like arms to embrace the edge of the woods. Horses, cows and other farm animals drank from a pond that glistened in the distance.

The front façade was of brilliant white oil paint, with two stories of tall English style windows trimmed with a medium brown color.

There was a driveway. A Dodge Ram pickup sat behind a Chevrolet Impala. Off to the side was a minibus. It was brown in color.

"That looks like the minibus," Ramsammy said as his eyes widened with alarm.

"You aren't kiddin' Alan."

Ramsammy pulled the Explorer off the highway. He parked the vehicle behind the Dodge Ram. The men got out the vehicle and seconds after, a young man stormed out a garage off to the side. He made his way to the lawmen with mincing steps.

"What can I do for you men?" the man asked, his voice raw with anger.

"We're detectives. I'm Detective Brogan and this is my partner, Detective Ramsammy," Martin Brogan said showing the man his badge. "Are you Frederick Ragnauth?"

"No. That's the boss. I work for him. My name's Paul Kumar," the man said as his implacable expression dissipated.

"We will like to see Mr. Ragnauth."

"May I ask for what reason?"

"Mr. Kumar, there's a police investigation that makes it necessary for us to see your boss," Ramsammy shot back, his mouth quirking in annoyance.

"OK. Okay sir. I mean no harm," the man responded as he scuttled away.

Minutes later the man returned.

"Are you both carrying guns?"

"Of course," Brogan answered. "We're cops aren't we?"

"You have to leave your guns with me if you want to see Mr. Ragnauth," the man replied as his face broke out in a cunning grin.

Brogan smiled defiantly. "Now you know that's not possible, my boy?"

"I'm not your boy, sir."

Brogan fixed the man with a stubborn stare.

"You're right on the money. We're sure of that. But the police chief in Georgetown has bestowed onto me all the rules I need to know. My partner and I made this trip to see Frederick Ragnauth, not you."

The man processed Brogan's words and tone in an irate way.

"Follow me!" he replied in a malicious voice.

The detectives followed the man through the front doorway into a large room. Tables, chairs and sofas were scattered loosely around a large television set. They followed the man into an adjoining room and waited as he knocked on a door.

"Come on in," bellowed a voice from inside.

The men went inside.

Frederick Ragnauth sat behind an untidy desk. A ceiling incandescent bulb threw a yellow glow of light across the dismal room. Ragnauth maintained a typical home office arrangement. Subtle signs of it being utilized occasionally was evident. The place was also used as a temporary area for keeping household items.

Ragnauth might have been in his mid-forties, with a head full of hair, an aquiline nose and a bushy boxcar mustache. When he rose to greet the detectives, he appeared to have been nearly six feet. Lanky with a sculpted face. His dungaree overall was clean, but his fingers were greasy. He whipped out a piece of tattered cloth from his pocket and ran it across his fingers. Then he reached over the desk and shook hands with the detectives and gestured them to take seats opposite his desk.

"Thank you, Kumar," he said to the man. "That will be all."

Paul Kumar shot the detectives a fierce, piercing look, then shook his head slightly.

"Okay, Mr. Ragnauth."

The detectives introduced themselves and stated their reason for coming to Ithaca. Martin Brogan showed Frederick Ragnauth a picture of the man they were hunting.

"Do you know this man?"

"Yes. That's the man I bought the minibus from."

"What's his name?"

"Walter Chattersingh."

"No. His real name is Mohan Basdeo."

"Really."

"That's for sure. Do you know the reason why the minibus you bought from him remains unregistered?"

"The motor vehicle department told me there was a hold on the registration but give no reason."

"More than that, the owner of that minibus is a suspect in a string of murders. The police want him for questioning."

"That dog!" Ragnauth shouted, his voice bitter with anger. "That's the reason he refused a check for the payment of the minibus. He insisted on cash. I paid him eight hundred thousand dollars in Guyana currency. I was shafted."

"All is not lost, Mr. Ragnauth. We will take the minibus in police custody until this matter is resolved," Ramsammy said.

"I break my balls everyday in the rice fields to make my money. It's not easy. That guy Basdeo is a scammer."

"We have a strong case against him, Mr. Ragnauth. Do you think he may be in Blairmont again?"

"Good question. That thug told me he was going to spend some time in New Amsterdam and eventually live with friends on the Corentyne Coast. The son-of-a-bitch could be anywhere."

"No doubt," Brogan answered.

CHAPTER 19

That afternoon, the detectives drove to Rosignol. They pulled the Ford Explorer on the ferry and crossed the Berbice River to New Amsterdam. By 5:00 p.m. the SUV was parked at 11 Strand Avenue at the Penguin International Hotel. The men secured the vehicle and entered the hotel lobby. They approached a woman behind a counter. She moved with businesslike precision as she worked on invoices.

"Good evening, gentlemen. I'm Ruby Calderia. May I help you?"

"Sure ma'am. We're detectives. I am Martin Brogan and this is my partner Alan Ramsammy," Brogan said as both men showed the woman their identification.

"What can I do to help?"

"We're looking to bed down for the night," Brogan said.

"One big room or two separate?"

"Two separate rooms, ma'am, with an adjoining door. You see, I watch the late show on TV. Don't want to disturb Mr. Brogan," Ramsammy chipped in.

"OK gentlemen," the woman answered going through her computer. "I've got two rooms on the second floor."

"That will be fine," Brogan said.

"Detectives, will you both take care of the bill yourselves?"

"No, Miss Calderia. You bill the Ministry of Home Affairs as per normal practice."

"OK. Just complete the registration and you'll be ready to go," the woman said. "By the way, we do have a restaurant and bar. Dinner is served at 8:00 p.m."

"Thank you, Miss Calderia. We sure can use some grub," Brogan said.

"One other question, ma'am," Alan Ramsammy said. "I've got something here," he said, placing a picture of Mohan Basdeo on the counter. "Have you seen this man?"

The woman picked up the picture and drew it close to her dimpled face. Her puffin-like eyes studied the image.

"No, detectives. I've never laid eyes on this man."

"Thank you, Miss Calderia."

The next day the detectives started early. They combed the city of New Amsterdam, interviewing clerks at the Astor Hotel on Strand Avenue, the Little Rock and the Parkway hotels on Main Street. They came up empty.

"So far Alan, we've checked four hotels. Mohan Basdeo never checked into any of them," Martin Brogan said.

"That's right. We still have to check out the Church View International. Who knows. We can hit pay dirt!" Ramsammy answered.

"One never knows. Let's grab something to bite on, then we'll pay a visit to that outfit on New Street."

Two hours later the Ford Explorer parked in front of the Church View, located at the corner of Main and New Streets.

Martin Brogan and his partner got out of the vehicle and walked towards the sprawling two-storied frame building. It was painted white with a tiled ground floor that was immaculately clean. The bar, restaurant and dining areas were situated in the rear, off to the left.

The detectives walked towards a box office where an elderly man was sitting at a desk.

"Hello, sir," Brogan said.

"Hello, looking for accommodation?"

"Not today. I'm Detective Brogan. This is my partner, Detective Ramsammy. Is there someone I can ask a few questions?"

"Sure. I'll get Harry Rattan for you. He's the manager and owner."

"Thank you."

The man made a call and within two minutes a man in his mid to late forties opened a door from a little office and approached the sleuths.

He was a dark-skinned Indo-Guyanese man, with black, billowing hair and an alligator smile. His right incisor was capped with gold. When he greeted the detectives, his laughter was improvised. Brogan introduced himself and his partner.

"Come in my office, Detectives," the man said after stating his name.

The men sat down behind a closed door. Ramsammy showed the man a picture of their quarry.

Harry Rattan looked at the picture. His eyes squinting.

"What's his name, Detective?"

"Accept my apology. My mistake. His name's Mohan Basdeo. But he goes by the name of Walter Chattersingh," Ramsammy admitted.

"This man was a guest in our hotel less than two weeks ago. He used the name Walter Chattersingh and was in Room 303 on the third floor," Harry Rattan said.

"Mr. Basdeo is a suspect in a triple murder investigation in Demerara," Brogan said. "We have to get any physical evidence he may have left behind."

"Since Mr. Basdeo left, the room was rented four times. The maids do a good job of cleaning up after every guest leaves. I don't see finding anything that Mr. Basdeo left in that room."

"I mean phone calls he might have made during his stay. Did he make any calls from his room?" Brogan asked.

The man accessed his computer and found the dates Mohan Basdeo stayed in Room 303.

"Mr. Basdeo paid a final bill of ten thousand five hundred dollars when he checked out of here last week. Five hundred dollars represented charges for using the hotel phone."

"How many calls did he make?"

"About two calls. You have to get that information from the telecommunications department in Georgetown. We have no details."

"I'm aware of that, Mr. Rattan. I want to thank you for being such a big help."

Brogan dived into his pocket and gave the man his business card. "If Mr. Basdeo or aka Chattersingh ever shows up here again, call me at that number."

"Will do just that, Detective. But there's one other thing Mr. Basdeo said to one of the maids when he left that morning."

"What did he say?" Brogan asked.

"He jokingly told her that when he gets to Crabwood Creek, he'll buy a palace and come back to the Church View for her."

"He must be a rich man," Ramsammy said.

"Must be, Detective. Only he knows," Harry Rattan replied.

"Mr. Rattan, I'm glad you mentioned what was said to the maid. It's important information for the police to know," Brogan added after a brief silence. "Don't forget to call me if you ever see this guy again."

"Sure will, Detective Brogan."

Brogan and his partner exited the building and got into the Explorer.

"That was some damn good information that guy Rattan finally gave us," Brogan said with a peremptory gesture.

"True. At least it gives us a place to start. Beats running around the countryside, looking for this freak."

"I think I know why he'll want to choose Crabwood Creek or Corriverton and not any other place."

"I see his rationale too. Both towns combined have a population of about twenty-five thousand people. Mostly Indo-Guyanese. The man can blend among his own race of people and be difficult to detect," Ramsammy reasoned.

"He might have thought of crossing the border to Suriname and laying low in Nikerie, Apoera or Matapi. But that will be difficult."

"Why you think so? He can cross the Corentyne River by speed boat," Ramsammy said.

"Easier said than done," Brogan added. "The smugglers will take all his money and his butt will be floating on the Corentyne River. Besides the Dutch Coast Guard are constantly on the move, ready to jack somebody's ass up who is trying to sneak into the country."

"Think I heard of those guys."

"Let's call Internal Affairs. Have them get some info from telecoms."

CHAPTER 20

The next day the Telecommunications Department in Georgetown sent an email to the police internal affairs located at Eve Leary. The letter stated that telecoms had traced two calls made from the Church View International Hotel to the Custom and Immigration department at Cheddi Jagan International Airport. The calls were made from Room 303 at about 4:30 a.m. Telecoms also noted that two days later, a call was made from the Hotel Mahogany in Corriverton, situated on the Corentyne Coast. The call was made a little before dawn to the same Custom and Immigration department as before but investigators were unable to locate a room at the Corriverton Hotel where the call originated.

Hours later Edgar Kilkenny, operations captain, at police headquarters in Brickdam got a copy of the email. With facial muscles tensing, he barked to his secretary to summon all detectives to the conference room immediately.

Later he stood before the ranks that included Detectives Brogan and Ramsammy who were assigned to the Basdeo investigation. His lightweight nylon jacket appeared a little rough and uneven, like it was stored in a duffel bag. His complexion leathery, as if he aged overnight.

He eyed the group piercingly. His voice sardonic.

"Thanks for being here in a timely manner gentlemen, for this ad hoc meeting. First, I want to congratulate everyone for his excellent detective work. A goal cannot be achieved in this type of work without a joint effort. I commend Detective Brogan and Ramsammy for their effort in locating a possible hideout for Mohan Basdeo. But our work has just begun. The fugitive may be in hiding in the Mahogany Hotel in downtown Corriverton or somewhere in that vicinity. He was last traced from the Church View International Hotel on New Street in New Amsterdam. Are there any questions?"

"I've got a question, Captain," a detective answered.

"Well go ahead. We don't have all day," Kilkenny blurted. "Ask your question!"

"What will be the next move?" the detective asked in a strangled voice.

"I was coming to that, Detective Wong. We've got to plant an undercover in the Mahogany. We've got to know the room Basdeo occupies if he's really there. Then we'll lure him out to ensure others' safety, then make an arrest or, worse case scenario, take him out if he shows hostility. We all know he's armed and dangerous."

"That's true, sir."

"Any other questions," Kilkenny asked, his voice stubborn, icy and defensive.

"One question for you, Captain."

"Go ahead, Ramsammy."

"There appears to be a link between a person or persons at the Custom and Immigration department at Cheddi Jagan Airport and the suspect. What's your take on that, Captain?"

"Good question. Right now we're working on that. When we get Basdeo, either dead or alive, we'll storm down to the airport. We know, based on those phone calls, he didn't act alone."

"Are we looking at a criminal enterprise here, Captain?" another rank asked.

"How on earth would I know! That's for you to figure out," Kilkenny scowled as his face tightened in annoyance. "But let me say this: Time is running out for those low-down pieces of dog dung. Sooner or later, the shit is going to hit the fan!" He ended his sentence as an insipid grin flashed across his face.

"Thank you, Captain," the rank responded.

"Any more questions?" Kilkenny asked, regarding his audience with a critical eye.

No one responded.

"You ranks, get outa here! Go give the bad guys more hell than a regular fellow could contemplate."

The following evening, a man of mixed race dressed in a business suit and carrying a suitcase, walked into the lobby at the Mahogany Hotel in Corriverton. He was about forty-two years old, hair cut short, with hawk-brown assuming eyes. He liked cricket, but at his age he figured he was too old to play. His feet were large and square. His curly, raven-colored hair was harshly brushed to the side of his head and his ears stood out like a fierce beast of prey. His hands were large and meaty with chapped, callused fingers and characteristically grease-stained nails. His suit was spun from blended cotton, wool and polyester. He sat down when he saw the clerk attending to another guest. In so doing, his pant legs hovered up, revealing an extraordinary pair of socks, made of wool, not nylon. Albeit Guyana's hot temperature.

He edged his way to the counter when the clerk gestured to him.

"May I help you, sir?"

"Looking for a room."

"How long is the stay?"

"Not sure. I'll do it one day at a time."

"OK, sir, please fill out this registration form."

"Sure, ma'am."

Five minutes later the man slid the completed form across the counter.

"Are you looking for a large or small room?"

"Small. A queen-sized bed will do just fine. It's just me."

"That will be fifteen hundred nightly."

"I can handle that price."

"Your room will be 209 on the second floor. Breakfast will be served at 8:00 a.m. and checkout time is 11:00 a.m. If you stay after 11:00 a.m., you'll be charged for another day."

"Sounds fair. Do you serve dinner?"

"Sure. It starts at 6:00 p.m. and ends at 9:00 p.m. It's 8:00 p.m. now. You've got an hour before the kitchen closes."

"Do I pay you now for my room?"

"No. When you're ready to leave you'll get a bill for everything including your meals."

"Thank you, ma'am. You've been so nice."

"It's my job, mister."

The man went to his room and showered. Then he donned a fiesta shirt and a pair of dungaree trousers. He made his way to the dining room and looked the people over, eying everyone with a delicate stare. Then he looked at the menu board. There was a special on for dinner that night. Dholl and rice with choka made from salted cod fish. He ordered the special and treaded by a table occupied by a young couple.

"Anyone sitting here?"

"No. Just us. Go ahead," the young man said.

"Thanks."

He ate his dinner in silence. Chewing slowly, then swallowing.

By 8:50 p.m. all of the hotel guests had left the dining room and gone to their rooms. Except one man who sat not too far from him. He was of Amerindian origin and bore a face unlike the one he was looking for.

Then the sudden ringing of his cell phone almost startled him. He fished the phone from his pocket as his eyes searched the dining room with caution. Quickly he stepped away from the hotel and got on the public road.

He answered his cell phone with a whisper.

"Hello."

"Leslie!"

"Hey Sergeant Harding."

"How is everything going?"

"Quiet, so far. I just came from the dining room in the hotel. I didn't see our man."

"He might have been in the dining room ahead of you and went back to his room."

"Possible. I got in the dining room half hour before closing time."

"In the morning, make sure you get in that dining room for breakfast. He's got to eat there unless he's on a starvation diet."

"I'll be there in the morning. Breakfast starts at 8:00 a.m. and ends at ten."

"Whatever you do, don't approach the man. Just make sure you've got a positive ID on him. I know you can handle him alone but don't break protocol."

"OK, Sergeant."

Leslie Turner was a member of the Guyana Police Force. He was stationed at the New Amsterdam constabulary on New Street when his supervisor notified him and other ranks that there was reason to believe that a murder suspect was said to be staying at the Mahogany Hotel in Corriverton.

The supervisor told his men that two detectives assigned to the case tracked the suspect to the Church View International Hotel. When they got to the hotel, the suspected murderer had already left. But records showed the man had made calls to the Customs and Immigration department at Cheddi Jagan Airport sometime before dawn while at the Church View Hotel. A call was also made to the airport from the Hotel Mahogany about the same hour of the morning. Thus there was ample reason to believe that Mohan Basdeo, the man sought by police, was living at the Hotel Mahogany under the name of Walter Chattersingh.

And it was late that evening when Leslie Turner got wind that Sergeant Harding wanted to see him in his New Amsterdam office the following morning.

"Good morning, Sergeant Harding," Officer Leslie Turner said as he entered the man's office.

"Nothin' good about the morning, Constable Turner. Just pull a chair and make yourself comfortable."

"OK, Sergeant."

"Yesterday I told you and other ranks that a murder suspect, Mohan Basdeo, aka Walter Chattersingh, may be in hiding at the Hotel Mahogany."

"Yes, sir. I'm well aware of that."

"Police Brass got together in Eve Leary at noon yesterday. They came up with a decision."

"What's that, Sergeant? Am I getting a medal if I were to get this guy?"

"No way, Constable. Don't allow your head to swell. But they named you as the man to work undercover at the Hotel Mahogany."

"To locate that crook."

"That's right. They know that the man is there. But they don't know the room he has as his burrow. Calling the hotel with that question will spook him."

"I'll be happy to take on the job, Sergeant Harding."

"Good. We're trying hard to avoid a shoot-out with this guy. He's got a criminal mind and we don't want to put the hotel guests in harm's way."

"I understand that, Sergeant."

"You're not new to this kind of job, Turner. I know you can kick some ass. You know the deal. Befriend the hoodlum when you get there. Find out his room number, then back off and leave the rest to those boys from Georgetown. Remember, country bumpkins like you and I don't go looking for trouble."

"Understand, sir."

"Now get outa here, Turner, and be safe. Don't come your butt back here in a body bag now."

"Course not, Sarge. When do I leave for Corriverton?"

"A police cruiser will drop you off after briefing at Corriverton Police at 4:00 p.m. today."

"Not a problem."

Leslie Turner was born in a place called Crabwood Creek. A small community on the Corentyne River about three miles from Corriverton. Turner, unlike most kids growing up in his town and attending high school in neighboring Corriverton, was considered an enigma by most of his classmates. His father was Afro-Guyanese and his mother was Amerindian. Descended from the Carib Tribe of Guyana's indigenous Indians.

Leslie had to fight off blustering, hostile and bullying bands of boys most days after school. Just because he appeared different. Grizzled black hair, a swarthy complexion and an exotic face. But deep within him was a burning desire to confront his adversaries, head to head. Without displaying a hint of fear.

That same determination followed him when he joined the Guyana Defense Force. And after two years, he rose to the rank of a sergeant major. He saw hostile action on Ankoko, a tiny Guyana territory, wedged between the Wenamu River and the mighty Cuyuni, bordering Venezuela. And again at Operteri against Dutch soldiers over a strategic border town.

And after ten years of being a soldier, he requested and got a transfer to the police force. It didn't take him long to be a member of the goon squad. Beating violent criminals into submission when they resisted being arrested or monitoring assigned areas during times of civil unrest.

Leslie Turner earned his reputation as an enforcer by virtue of his brutality and his propensity to confront his foes. To him, engaging a man holding up in a hotel room was nothing more than a walk in the park. He figured on barging through that door and shattering the man's bones. But he knew that such a conduct would not be condoned by the police department.

CHAPTER 21

Tuesday morning was a fine Corriveron day, Leslie Turner reckoned when he came down to the dining room in the Mahogany Hotel. He got a cup of coffee and two slices of buttered toast and took a chair in the far corner of the eating area. From his position, he ransacked the locality with arrogant, impassive eyes.

About a dozen people were dining. Talking and laughing. Men, women and children. Mohan Basdeo was not among the mix.

Leslie Turner downed three cups of coffee while waiting for a man he'd never met. Nine thirty came and went. The dining room was to be shuttered at 10:00 a.m. Turner ordered another coffee and nursed it until the place was closed for breakfast.

He walked through the lobby and exited the front door. Then he lit a cigarette and strolled along the pavement on the main drag. The day turned out to be a hot one, Turner figured. Fifteen minutes later he returned. He opened the door to the hotel lobby and entered. Turner felt as though the world outside was in flames. The leaves of the big mango tree situated behind the Mahogany Hotel hung rigid. Not a breeze trespassed through them in the stunning heat. But yet they teemed with life.

Leslie Turner retreated to his room. Twelve forty five p.m. found him sitting on a chair next to his table. Cabin fever was catching up to him. He made his way down the stairs and towards the dining area. The smell of food hit him with a quick slap in the face. The place was crawling with hotel guests who figured on getting a bite to eat before lunchtime came to an end.

In the center of the dining room was a wall. It did not look important. Built of particle board and finished at the borders with roughly cut molding. Guests eating were able to look above it and beyond. Furthermore, it could be clambered over by a child. There was no gate to move from one side to the other. The idea of a gate was not evident when locomotion was a practical alternative.

To Leslie Turner, that idea was real. On the other side of the wall where other people dined, was a man who caught his attention. A man in his fifties with a full beard and a savage face.

Turner got his meal from the server and walked to the side of the wall where the man was seated. He sat by a table with close proximity to the stranger.

"Hello there," Turner said.

"Hey," the man answered in a voice heavy with enmity.

"How's the food?"

"I've eaten better meals, mister. This crap is just to allay my hunger."

"I hear you. I'm hungry myself."

"Can't wait to get to hell out of here and eat some real good food. Not this shit!"

"Reckon you're right. There must be better food someplace else."

"Sure. But who are you, mister? You look rather clean cut like a Georgetown politician."

Leslie Turner looked into the man's eyes before answering. He knew he was sitting close to Mohan Basdeo aka Walter Chattersingh. A picture he bore in his pocket was a dead ringer of the man wanted by police. His withered, time worn face told Turner that he was a man who was not a stranger to trouble or he might have always been engaged in conflict. Deep in his countenance there was a subtle undercurrent of hostility. His brawny and hairy limbs suspended from his torso like exaggerated appendages. His black-bearded jaw, stubborn as a nutcracker, hung clumsily on his face.

"No, sir. Never was a politician and never will be."

"What's your business, man?"

"Salesman. Work for Alesi, a rice importer based in Nickerie. What do you do?"

"Rice farmer from Port Mourant."

"Great. Not every day a man runs into a rice farmer. We do have something in common."

"True. My name's Chattersingh. You can call me Walter."

"I'm James Cordis."

"When again are you going back to Suriname, James?"

"In a couple of days. Do you know people in Nickerie?"

"No. Just want to go for a visit."

"Are you taking the ferry boat across the pond?"

"No. I'd rather cross the river by speed boat."

"That's not impossible."

"Know anyone with a speed boat? I'll pay him well."

"Yes, I know someone. But I'll have to get back to you with that information."

"How soon will that be, James? I'll like to be in Nickerie as soon as possible. You may not understand."

"In that case, I will give the guy a call sometime today. I'll tell you what he says when I see you here at dinnertime."

"Thank you, man. I really appreciate you hooking me up with this guy."

"Walter, I can see you're not so bad a fellow. I'll do my best to help you at anytime."

"Thanks man, James. That's what I want to hear. What room they got you in?"

"Two hundred nine on the second floor."

"I'm not too far from you in Room 217, further down the hall."

"Well, hold tight. Give me a couple of hours and I'll have some information for you after I speak to the man who got the speed boat."

"Good idea," the man said as his face erupted in an incriminating grin.

For a quick moment, Turner gazed in the man's face. It was marked by hanging skin folds, yellow tobacco-stained teeth, pitted with cavities. He knew Basdeo had no idea whatsoever that he was undercover. And soon the chips were going to fall.

The chair creaked under the burden of his two-hundred-pound frame when Basdeo moved his body in his effort to stand.

"Later, James," Basdeo said as he looked around him with probing eyes.

Turner watched the man tread across the dining room floor and up to his room. He sneered inwardly at him. Because he knew that for him, the end of the road was near. Mohan Basdeo aka Walter Chattersingh was about to swallow, hook and sinker.

CHAPTER 22

At 8:00 p.m. that evening a knock came to the door of Room 217 at the Mahogany Hotel. It was sudden and quick, like the drumming of a woodpecker on a balata tree.

"Who is there?" a voice exploded, as if in panic.

"Walter. It's me, James Cordis."

"James, is that you? Let me open the door."

Inside the man made his way across the room in order to open the door. He was sweating. His entire anatomy looked gluey as his extremities blossomed with goose bumps. His throat became dry as if baked by a desert sun. Mohan! What in hell is going on? he asked himself. You aren't a darn teenager anymore. You are in your fifties. A grown-ass man. You faced cops, knives and bad guys on the streets and survived for months at a time in a raunchy minibus. Leaving the comfort of his room to head out with a stranger was nothing more than a cake walk, he told himself. He felt it was something that had to be done. Leaving Corriverton and heading out to Nickerie would ensure his safety and longevity. A good move, you jackass, he reasoned. You wanted this for a long time. Did you not?

Quickly Basdeo opened the door.

"Come in, James. What you've got for me?"

"Good news, Walter. My friend will be here with his car at 8:30 p.m. I take it that you're dressed and ready."

"Yes. I just hopped from the shower and pulled my clothes on."

"True. You look a little wet, Walter."

"A little. Now where is your friend taking me?"

"A few miles from here. Number 76 Village."

"Is that far?"

"About three miles from Corriverton. He's got a landing dock in his backyard in 76 Village."

"Good, man. How much he'll charge me?"

"His price is six thousand to take you across the Corentyne River. Can you handle that price, Walter?"

"Sure. I don't have a problem with that."

"Well, let's go. It's eight twenty."

Basdeo grabbed his suitcase and pulled the door shut when the men exited the room. They shuffled down the stairs to the first floor. Basdeo stopped at the front office. A clerk sitting behind a long counter gave the men a cautious stare.

"Are you men checking out?"

"I am," Basdeo said. "Room 217."

The clerk checked her computer and gazed up at Basdeo after printing out his final bill.

"That's it, sir."

Basdeo paid the woman in Guyana currency he fished from his pocket.

"Thank you, Mr. Chattersingh," the clerk said politely. "We'll be happy to have you again."

Basdeo did not answer the woman but he flashed her a superficial smile.

The men exited the lobby of the Mahogany Hotel and walked towards the street. A red Nissan Pathfinder was sitting by the sidewalk.

"Is this the vehicle?" Basdeo asked.

"Yes, Calvin is here. Right on time," Leslie Turner said.

The driver of the Nissan was a tall man in his thirties with shaggy black hair and a symmetrical face. One would say that he was not the kind of fellow who wanted to be in a place where he was at that time of night. But there he was. He could not deny that where he was going was unfamiliar nor were the details fuzzy.

The man got from the vehicle and walked around its front. He met Turner and the other man by the left passenger door.

"Hey, James. Glad I'm able to make it tonight," the driver said as he eyed the men with a calm look on his face and being careful not to blow Turner's cover.

"Thanks, Calvin. This is the man you're taking across the river," Turner said.

The driver turned and looked at Basdeo.

"My name's Calvin Ramchal. Glad to help you."

"Thanks. The name is Walter."

"OK, Walter. Load up and let's go."

"I'll hop along for the ride," Turner said.

"Sure, I'll bring you back to the hotel," Calvin Ramchal answered.

Calvin Ramchal started the vehicle and made a U-turn, leaving Corriverton and the Mahogany Hotel in his rearview mirror.

Leslie Turner was seated in the rear of the Nissan while Basdeo sat next to the driver. From his vantage point, Turner was able to observe the man's every move.

It was 9:00 p.m. Darkness hugged the land in its subtle embrace. Moments of silence gripped the Nissan as it left Corriverton's city limits.

The vehicle approached Number 76 Village. Street lights were nowhere. Calvin Ramchal put the pedal to the metal as the Nissan exceeded seventy miles per hour.

Suddenly from a quiet cross street, a siren blared. Ramchal looked into his rearview mirror. Two police cruisers with flashing blue lights were in hot pursuit.

"Man. I'll be damned!" Calvin Ramchal croaked.

"Maybe you were speeding," Turner said.

"Yes. Indeed I was speeding. Everybody stay cool. I'll talk my way out of this," the driver said.

"Will everything be OK, Mr. Ramchal?" Basdeo asked the driver with a face lost in speculation.

"Leave everything to me. I never realized that cops will be on the highway at this time of night."

"Shit happens sometimes," Basdeo said in an irate tone of voice.

"No doubt," Calvin Ramchal answered.

Within minutes a brazen voice came from the loudspeaker of the first police car.

"Pull over to the left, now!"

The intensity of the sound ricochetted in the darkness. Calvin Ramchal followed the instruction from the police cruiser. He pulled the Nissan to the right of the highway and killed the engine.

Within seconds, four ranks stomped out of the two squad cars. With flashlights in hand and boots reverberating the asphalt highway, they scrambled towards the Nissan.

"Let us see your hands!" rapacious voices bellowed out. The lead cop was badger-faced, with a wide hip and a booming Berbician voice. He made his way to the driver's side.

"Do you know why you were stopped, Mister?" he asked Calvin Ramchal with a growl as the other ranks beamed their flashlights at the car.

"No, sir," Ramchal said politely.

"You were speeding. Besides one of your back lights is out of order."

"Wasn't aware of that, Officer."

"Show me your driver's license and registration for this vehicle."

Calvin Ramchal dug into his shirt pocket and came up with some papers.

"Here they are, Officer."

The lead cop took the papers from Ramchal and studied them acutely. Then he fixed the other two men with eyes sharpening.

"Your IDs, gentlemen."

"Got to get mine from my suitcase," Basdeo said as a spasm crossed his face.

"Go ahead, mister, get your ID," the lead rank told the man. But suddenly Basdeo opened the passenger door and dashed into the night. In his haste to evade the police, he crashed into a barbed wire fence along the highway. He cried out in a voice raw with anguish as the sharp metals penetrated his skin. But the ranks were hot on his trail.

"We got you now, Mr. Basdeo!" the lead rank shouted. "All these men here are police officers. You were duped into thinking that they were taking you across the pond."

Mohan Basdeo heard the cop after he hauled his body over the fence. The area was unknown to him and despite his injury, he dragged his battered body along. He looked over his shoulder again and again as he prowled through the low bushes with labored breath. And red hot with rage. That he was outsmarted by a bunch of two-bit ranks, caused his face to be etched in fury. His eyes penetrated the evening gloom. About a mile ahead, he peered wildly at a grove of coconut palm. Basdeo tried to run faster. He had to conceal his impaired body in their clotted boughs. The barking of the irate dogs thundered against his eardrums. Notwithstanding, he scampered along. Then an outcrop root suddenly caught at his foot. It sent him scattering on his hands and knees. But like a cornered wild beast, he regained his feet. His muscles throbbed. He felt he had to pretend that the pain was not there. Mind over matter, he grumbled.

Sweat streamed into his eyes! He wiped it away as the clamor of angry police dogs got closer. Only if he had his gun. Why was he such a moron to pack it away in his suitcase. And of all places, in a police cruiser.

But then, he had no choice. He had to forge ahead in a haze of terror.

Without reaching the coconut palms, Basdeo felt himself reeling sideways and forward. He was slowing down. His breath and energy appeared to be sagging simultaneously. Again he stumbled. That time on his stomach and abdomen. And the tracking dogs were upon him.

"Cuff that bastard!" a caustic voice rang out. "He's going back to Georgetown in chains." Fear and a sudden crushing surge of hopelessness jolted Basdeo's brain.

"Help me, you fools. Get these friggin' dogs away. They're goin' to kill me!"

Quickly, Mohan Basdeo was placed in leg irons and handcuffs.

By then, other members of the task force converged on the scene. Martin Brogan and his partner Alan Ramsammy were amongst them.

The ranks removed the suitcase that was found in the Pathfinder, being careful not to distort the physical evidence.

"Sergeant, look what we have here," an officer cringed in astonishment after the case was opened. "There's a ton of money here!"

"That's probably the money the suspect got when he sold the minibus to that fellow in Ithaca," the sergeant responded.

"Yes, sir," said another rank. "There's also a gun here and about forty rounds of ammo."

"What sort of gun, Constable?" the sergeant asked.

"Looks like a thirty eight caliber revolver."

"Shit! Must be the weapon used to kill those people."

"Good possibility."

"You fellows bag that stuff. It's compelling evidence. Someone get the detectives over here pronto."

Brogan and his sidekick inventoried the evidence and walked over to the paddy wagon where Basdeo was held. Alan Ramsammy opened the door of the vehicle. The detectives eyed the man as his face bore a stony expression.

"I'm Detective Brogan and this is my partner, Alan Ramsammy. You must be Mohan Basdeo. Are you not?"

"No! You shit-for-brains. I'm the Lord Mayor of Georgetown! What do you jerks want with me?"

"Mr. Basdeo," Brogan answered politely. "I've got a picture of you right here. Is this person not you?"

"To hell with you numbskulls. I'm Walter Chattersingh. Don't have a clue as to what you're talking about or who that cocksucker is in that picture."

"We know that you're Mohan Basdeo from the East Coast," Alan Ramsammy added. "But regardless of who on earth you say you are, you still will be charged with the murders of three people."

"You have to prove that, pretty boy!" Basdeo lashed out with his face bearing a defiant grin.

"Mr. Basdeo, if you give us the names of others who are involved in this, maybe the crown prosecutor may want to cut you a deal," Brogan said. "This is some serious shit. If a court of law finds you guilty, that young woman judge from Berbice will hang your ass till your eyes pop out!"

"Don't know what you're talkin' about," Basdeo answered as his face tensed up.

"Man, don't feed me that bullshit, like you don't know what on earth I'm tellin' you!"

"Go to hell, Detective Brogan. Both you and your beetle-faced partner got nothin' on me!"

"Basdeo, let me say this and I'll give it to you straight fella, no beating about the bush and that old-time shit!" Brogan muttered as he ground out his words between clenched teeth. "Brickdam's got hard evidence on your ass. From Le Repentir Cemetery in Georgetown to the Mahogany in Corriverton. You'll help yourself if you start calling names."

"I need a lawyer," Basdeo answered frigidly.

"That doesn't mean a thing. You're a dead man sitting," Ramsammy said boldly.

"Even if I'm a dead man walking, I still need a friggin' lawyer!" Basdeo shouted with nostrils flaring. "I have nothin' to say."

"That's your right, fella," Brogan snapped, "but even the best attorney in Georgetown will catch hell getting you out of this one."

"You're as stubborn as they come, mister," Alan Ramsammy said.

"Don't know what you're talkin' about," Mohan Basdeo answered as he regarded the detectives with snobbish horror.

"I've got to know the answer to another question," Brogan said as he looked into the man's red, irritated and oppressive eyes.

"Go ahead, Detective. I'm all ears," Basdeo said, croaking out his words in strangled tones.

"You made calls to Cheddi Jagan International Airport while you stayed at the Church View and the Mahogany Hotels. Am I right?"

"Like hell you're right, sucker!"

"Who is the person you spoke to?"

"None of your damn business!"

"It's my business, mister. As a detective, I've got a right to know," Brogan answered.

"Let's say I got friends in high places."

"Well, give us some names!"

"Never. I'm not as dumb as you think."

"Come on, Mr. Basdeo. Were they involved with you? Those cats are walking and you're the fall guy!"

"I have nothin' more to say, Detective," Basdeo said in a huff.

"We'll see you in Georgetown, man!" Brogan said making an angry dismissive gesture.

CHAPTER 23

In the days following Mohan Basdeo's arrest, September had turned out to be awfully rainy. Georgetown saw deluge after deluge of thunderstorms. The city was reduced to nothing but a landscape of boggy and swampy streets. An unforgettable quagmire, where even the boldest refused to tread.

Crime, too, stayed indoors with the rain. The choke-and-rob incidents, street corner assaults, vandalisms and domestic violence, all took a time out, where marauding flood waters hit the hardest.

That morning, Edgar Kilkenny, Brickdam Operation Captain, ushered about fifteen rank into the conference room. The group included Detectives Brogan and Ramsammy. Brogan glanced at the man's face. It bore a buoyant mood, he imagined. Something uncharacteristic for a man he knew for decades.

"I would not repeat to you ranks what you already know. A task force that was set up on the Corentyne nabbed Mohan Basdeo two days ago. The man was said to be armed and dangerous and is the main suspect in three murders."

"Why was Mr. Basdeo not taken into custody by the undercover rank at the Mahogany?" a young constable asked.

"Good question, constable," Kilkenny replied. "How long are you a policeman, son?"

"One year, Captain," the man answered.

"You will learn in this job that protecting the public is just as important as you'll protect yourself. We, the police, try our best to keep the public out of harm's way when a man as dangerous as Mohan Basdeo is on the loose with a gun. We knew our quarry was holed up in a hotel room in Corriverton, but we did not attempt to kick the door down to get him. That would have been like cornering a cat. It will strike back. So we have to commend all the ranks involved in that manhunt for defusing a dangerous situation. A criminal was apprehended and nobody was hurt," Kilkenny said as a silly, self-conscious, tight-lipped and affected smile crossed his countenance. "Any other questions?"

"Yes, Captain Kilkenny," a police interrogator said. "I've got a question."

"Go ahead, Sergeant. What's on your mind?"

"My partner and I questioned Mr. Basdeo for hours yesterday. He refused to give the name or names of the people he called from the hotels in Berbice. He's adamant about implicating anyone and denied knowledge of the murders. What's the next move?"

"Physical evidence that was collected, will put a nail in his coffin. You know something Sergeant. Basdeo thinks he's slick. We got other investigators questioning him right now as we speak. And it's gonna go on day and night until we crack his butt. Even if we've got to squeeze his balls or waterboard his stinkin' ass. We'll go that far. But don't worry, that bastard will tell before we're through with him."

"Got you, Captain."

"Anybody else has a question to ask?"

A silence came over the conference room before Kilkenny spoke again. "Later today Detectives Brogan and Ramsammy will head out to Cheddi Jagan International Airport for some investigative work. We have to get some clues on the person or persons Basdeo called when he was in Berbice. I'll see both men in my office for briefing."

One hour later Martin Brogan and his partner left police headquarters in Brickdam and headed out to the airport.

"What do you make of Kilkenny today?" Alan Ramsammy was the first to speak after getting in the driver's seat.

"Got no words to describe that joker. Guess he's just plain grumpy."

"That's undeniable. But he wasn't such a pain in the butt today. He wasn't trying to belittle anyone."

"Right. He was tryin' hard to be nice."

"Maybe he got laid last night."

"Hell, no. I guess that man doesn't have any libido left in him. Let alone getting it up."

"That's why the man is so miserable, Martin. Look at his face. He's always looking pissed off."

"He's the boss. Let's get to that airport and follow his orders."

"Do we have a choice?" Ramsammy asked.

"No friggin' way."

It was 10:30 a.m. when the Ford Explorer pulled into a parking lot at Cheddi Jagan International Airport. Martin Brogan tossed his Guyana Police plaque on the dashboard. He checked his shoulder holster. His weapon was secure. He glanced at his wristwatch. Ten thirty three.

The detectives crossed the wide expanse of the asphalt-paved surface. By weaving between parked vehicles, light poles and stationary security barriers. They moved resolutely up a concrete footpath and entered an automatic doorway that led to the terminals.

The detectives sat in the rear of a small coffee shop and ordered breakfast. Brogan glanced around at the other patrons. Their faces showed oblivion to the casually dressed men who sipped black coffee and nibbled on buttered toast with bacon and scrambled eggs.

"Just find it hard to remember the name of the man we've got to see," Ramsammy said.

"I've got it written here," Brogan said pulling a notepad from his pocket. "I wrote it down after we left Kilkenny's office. It's Brandon Dalrymple."

"Yes. That's him."

"He's the man running Customs and Immigration at the airport. He knows everyone on the other shifts."

"Fine. That makes our job easier."

"Time will tell. Ready when you are."

"I'm with you, Boss."

The detectives crossed a busy floor and ascended a flight of stairs. They came to a polished mahogany door with the letters Customs and Immigration. Brogan opened the door to an air-conditioned office. A middle-aged woman with a judgmental expression on her face was sitting behind a computer. She sported a dark-brown pantsuit that was far greater than her size.

"May I help you men?"

"Yes, ma'am. I'm Detective Brogan. This is my partner, Alan Ramsammy," Brogan said as both detectives flashed their badges. "We're here to see Mr. Dalrymple."

"Was he expecting you?"

"Sure. Our captain in Brickdam had notified him of our coming," Brogan said.

"OK. I'll tell him."

The woman went to an adjoining office and opened the door. "Mr. Dalrymple, two detectives are here to see you," she said in a strangled voice.

"Send them in please, Miss Wright. I'm aware of their coming," came the sound of a ponderous voice.

The detectives entered the opened door and came face to face with a man standing behind a desk with an outstretched hand.

"It's a pleasure, Detectives," the man named Dalrymple said while shaking their hands. He was a diminutively built Portuguese fellow about five-feet-three, about fifty-five, with a thick head of wiry hoarfrost hair and eyes red as a python's, suggesting to the lawmen that he hit the bottle without remorse. His harsh gravel-like voice was incongruous to his size, but it matched his bloodshot eyes and his rugged handshake.

Dalrymple led the lawmen through another door to a seating area with four chairs and a coffee table. "I don't know about you detectives," he began, "but for me it's time for my third cup of coffee," Dalrymple said as he walked over to a table that had a brewed pot with packets of sugar, creamers and spoons.

"I already had my coffee, Mr. Dalrymple," Brogan said in an apologetic tone, "but thanks to you anyway."

"That makes two of us," Ramsammy added.

Brandon Dalrymple took a mouthful of his coffee and returned to his chair.

"So what can I do for you detectives?"

"We're here seeking information into a murder investigation," Martin Brogan said.

"Are you serious, Detective Brogan?"

"Never more serious, Mr. Dalrymple. We have a suspect in custody. Our investigation has shown that while on the loose, he made some phone calls to Customs and Immigration in the wee hours of the morning."

"What? When was this?"

"These are the dates and time. This is the number our suspect called."

Brandon Dalrymple pulled the sheet of paper closer to him and studied the information as his eyes blinked with incredulity.

"This phone number is in the supervisor's office on the main floor. The person in charge handles issues relating to domestic and international flights."

"Who is this supervisor, Mr. Dalrymple?" Brogan asked.

"I've got about six supervisors there. Two on each shift. One is always there when the other is off either on vacation or weekends."

"Let's narrow this down to the morning of the date indicated on that sheet of paper. How many supervisors were on and what were their names?"

Brandon Dalrymple went back to his office with the detectives in tow. He accessed his computer to the date indicated by Brogan.

"There was one supervisor working those mornings in question," Dalrymple said as his eyes focused on the computer.

"Who was that supervisor, Mr. Dalrymple?"

"A man named Joseph Pollard."

"Do other employees have access and authorized to use that phone in Mr. Pollard's office?"

"No, Detective Brogan. Employees screening passengers coming to Guyana may call that phone for a supervisor when and if there's a problem."

"What are examples of some of the problems that an employee may call his supervisor?"

"Passport or visa problems with passengers?"

"That's all?"

"No. Also not declaring to customs the correct amount of foreign currency one has in his possession."

"So customs and immigration has to know the amount of currency a passenger is bringing into the country?"

"Yes. It's the law of the land. Not only that. We also have to get an address or where he's going to stay."

"Thank you, Mr. Dalrymple," Brogan said.

"I hope I was able to assist you, Detective."

"Sure. Your help was invaluable."

"Thanks, Detective Brogan."

"Here's my card. Call me if you need me, Mr. Dalrymple."

CHAPTER 24

It was 2:45 p.m.

Brogan and his partner Alan Ramsammy filed out across the dismal stretch of the parking lot and got into the Ford Explorer.

The temperature was brutal. Alan Ramsammy cranked the engine and pulled down the windows. A stubborn heat hung in the SUV. Some relief came when the driver got on the main pike and headed towards Georgetown.

"Looks like we got the big fish," Ramsammy said.

"Who knows? But later on we've got to pay Mr. Pollard a visit. He's the supervisor working tonight."

"What if he denies knowing Basdeo?"

"He will. I anticipate that he'll deny any knowledge of Basdeo. That's why Kilkenny did not allow the media to know that Basdeo was in custody," Brogan said.

"That would've scared Pollard if he heard that Basdeo was in police custody. He will be fearful that his buddy is going to rat on him."

"Don't worry, Alan. When I see Mr. Basdeo later, I'll throw a bouncing ball at his ass."

"I figure you will," Ramsammy said as a restrained laughter ruffled his face.

Twelve hours later, the detectives pulled the Ford Explorer to a stop in the parking lot at Cheddi Jagan International Airport. Brogan threw his police decal on the dashboard and double parked next to an airport security vehicle. The forever chirping of grasshoppers and other night crawlers was loud among the shrubbery that lined the footpath.

The detectives approached the building and entered the airlines checkout area. British West Indian Airlines was the only carrier opened and operating in full swing. Arrived passengers and their luggage were searched at a checkout point by customs employees while four airport security guards eyed the operation with feral-like precision. A small weekday morning crowd was gathered behind a protective barrier. It's occupants peered about the customs area, wild-eyed looking for familiar faces.

Brogan and his partner followed a roped off area to the right. They had little trouble finding their destination. Supervisor of Customs and Immigration. Ramsammy tapped gently on the door. A few moments elapsed before the huge metal door swung inward and opened. Its hinges uttering a sound of contempt. Then a man, as big as a refrigerator, occupied the doorway. He eyed the detectives with unconcealed rancor. The man stood a good six—feet, vast through the chest, with rippling partly exposed biceps under a short-sleeved shirt.

The detectives looked into his face. They noticed the roguish expression and unflinching jaw. Brogan, in all his years as a cop, never before felt the way he was feeling. The sensation of a spider crawling up his back, as his heart hammered against his breast plate. Quickly and subtly, he took a deep breath. No one noticed. He swallowed his feelings with embarrassment and quickly realized that he, and he alone, was conscious of his fear.

Brogan affected a businesslike smile. "Good morning," he said in a pleasant manner. "I believe you're Joseph Pollard, aren't you?"

The man rolled his eyes piercingly from one detective to the other. Eyes dark and frigid, as if lacking moisture. When he spoke, his words spluttered out in a whiskey-roughened fume.

"Yes, I'm Joseph Pollard."

"I'm Detective Brogan. This is my partner Alan Ramsammy," Brogan said showing the man his badge.

"What's this about, Detective?"

"We got a man behind bars in Georgetown for the murders of three people. They passed through this airport," Brogan explained as a pleasant calm came over him.

"What in hell that has to do with you seeing me?"

"A lot, Mr. Pollard."

"Meaning what?"

"The man said he knows you, Mr. Pollard. You and him are buddies. You did work together," Brogan said as his eyes hardened.

"Who is this cocksucker anyway?"

"A fellow named Mohan Basdeo," Brogan said, bringing a picture to the man's eye level. Joseph Pollard glanced at the picture as if showing no interest.

"Never saw that ugly buzzard. Detective Brogan, why would you think of me being as inglorious as to even be linked to a man like that?"

"You tell me, Mr. Pollard. Mr. Basdeo claims he called you on this telephone number on more than one occasion while he was hiding from police."

"Detective, have you examined that man's head? I have no knowledge of what you're alleging."

"Mr. Pollard, according to records, I can place you in this office, right here in the wee hours of that morning when those calls came in," Brogan retorted.

"Someone here is not playing with a full deck, Detective."

"Is anyone else authorized to use this telephone on your desk, Mr. Pollard?"

"Not that I know of."

"You're the supervisor here, sir. Don't you know what's goin' on in this office?"

"I never said I didn't, Detective Brogan. Everyone here knows that I run a tight ship."

"Mr. Pollard, someone is lying like hell. Either you or Basdeo. But time will tell. Stay as you are for now, but in time, we'll be calling you down to the Timehri police station to make a statement of what you know. We've got to leave now. But we'll be back."

Joseph Pollard's eyes widened incredulously. His thoughts were spiraling out of control like he was about to experience a panic attack. That friggin' Basdeo. He should have rubbed him out a long time ago. Pollard fought for self control. It brought sweat to his brow during his momentary muse.

"Whatever you say, Detective," Joseph Pollard grumbled as his mouth crimped in annoyance. "Close the friggin' door behind you, if you please."

Brogan and his partner left the building and walked towards the SUV. Brogan was the first to speak.

"I should have put some handcuffs on that damn loud mouth."

"Good idea. But that won't hold good with the Crown Prosecutor."

"I see your point, Alan. Lack of probable cause."

"True. No reason to arrest him."

"But now I think I can see the big picture surrounding this investigation."

"How so?"

"Pollard, Basdeo, and maybe others are engaged in a criminal enterprise."

"I know there's a connection somewhere."

"When people pass through customs, they have to declare their monies, valuables and whatever they have in their possession to the intake officer. Also their addresses. I believe the intake officer funnels information of someone with a lot of money and other possessions to Joseph Pollard."

"I see where you're headed, Martin. I got the idea."

"Correct. Pollard contacts Mohan Basdeo with the description of the passenger."

"So Basdeo waits in the parking area with his minibus and offers the passenger a ride to his destination for far less money than other minibuses are charging."

"Yes, Alan. You've got the idea. Basdeo kills the passenger, dumps or buries the body and splits the spoils with Joseph Pollard and others."

"So what follows is what we already know."

"That's for sure. But the only way we can get Pollard into custody is if Basdeo points a finger at him."

"True. We can't arrest him based on the phone calls that went to his office. As per law, we need hard evidence to haul that prick in."

"Once we reign him in, I'm sure he'll give up the name of the intake officer."

"That will be in his best interest."

Alan Ramsammy got in the driver's seat and pulled the vehicle on the main highway as it headed to Georgetown. It was 5:10 a.m. Morning twilight was taking shape as a kaleidoscope of colors transformed the eastern horizon. Bat falcons, red-tailed night hawks and ash-colored swifts darted about the sky.

The detectives sat in silence for a short period, each in his own thoughts. Ramsammy pondered his feelings of uncertainty and ambivalence to face marriage. Thoughts of him and the woman occupying his bed had begun to nibble at him some time ago. He was the first to speak.

"I wanted to mention something to you, Martin."

"What's that man?"

"It's Julie and I."

"Problems?"

"Of sorts. Two days ago she asked me about marriage."

"That's serious. What did you say?"

"I told her that I wasn't ready."

"I know that pissed her off."

"Right. She got mad as hell and told me she cannot go on like the way she was because most of her friends are married."

"Alan, you've got to tell her something that will give her hope. If not, she'll walk out on you. That's if you want to continue with her."

"I love the woman, Martin. We've been together for years. I don't want to lose her but once I get married, it's like being tied down."

"Bullshit man! You're hog-tied now. Aren't you?"

"In a way."

"Well, you've got to get serious about life. Sometime. Some day. Do you think Julie is worthy to be your wife?"

"Sure. No question about that."

"You got some talkin' to do when you get to your house."

"Looks that way, Martin. How are you and your lady doing?"

"Fantastic man. Good food. Great sex. I'm in love with the woman."

"Good for you."

"Life sometimes can be so unfair, Alan."

"What you mean?"

"A man lost his life due to another man's depravity and another gains his woman."

"That makes the world go around, Martin."

"Guess so, partner."

CHAPTER 25

The next day the detectives met with Edgar Kilkenny in his Brickdam office. The man flashed them an improvised grin exhibiting a mouthful of ill-fitting dentures.

"So talk to me, detectives. What did you learn from Joseph Pollard?"

"He's playing hardball. Said he didn't know what we were talking about," Brogan answered.

"Is that so? Well, we'll continue to burst his balls. He'll come up with something."

"Captain, one can tell the man is lying," Ramsammy added.

"We all know that Pollard is not coming up with the facts. We've got to find a way to nail his butt."

"I think we can do that, Captain," Brogan said with an assertive expression on his face.

"Detective, you've got to do what you have to do to put some handcuffs on that sleaze ball and all others involved with him."

"I hear you, Captain."

"The other ranks interrogating Basdeo were not successful in getting anything out of him. They have been at it for a week. That jive turkey has been saying that we have the wrong man."

"Then who's the right guy? Did he say who was the right man?" Brogan asked without showing any emotion.

"Course not," Kilkenny said.

"Today, Alan and I will see Basdeo for the fourth time for an interrogation session."

"Use whatever method you want to, Detective Brogan. Pull the friggin' rabbit out of the hat. Work some magic and let this man talk."

"I'm optimistic."

"That's what I want to hear. The brass in Eve Leary are looking for closure in this crap."

It was 11:30 a.m. Brogan and his partner grabbed themselves coffee from a small kitchen area located in the precinct, then they moved to the area where Basdeo was in custody.

"You cocksuckers again!" Basdeo shouted in a brazen voice after looking up and seeing the detectives.

"We've got some new information on you man."

"That shit is not new anymore, Detective."

The rank on duty watching the man in custody got from his desk and unlocked the cell. Another rank secured Basdeo with handcuffs and walked him over to the interrogation room.

The detectives closed the door behind them and the man in custody sat in a chair.

"Listen good, Mr. Basdeo. The Crown Prosecutor is getting ready to put you on trial for the murder of three former Guyanese coming back for a visit. It appears as if you alone want to take on this rap although others may be involved. That I cannot comprehend. I also want you to know that this conversation is being recorded."

"Don't give a monkey's ass. Besides I don't know what you're talkin' about."

"Detective Ramsammy and I spoke to a man working with Customs and Immigration at Cheddi Jagan International Airport yesterday."

"That doesn't mean anything to me."

"Sure it does, Basdeo."

"Why you think so?"

"He identifies you as the trigger man."

"What! You're bullshitting me!"

"I'm not kidding. A man named Joseph Pollard identified you as the shooter."

"That douche bag," Basdeo screamed as he shot upright in his chair. "We had an understanding. That fellow and I had a deal."

"Guess what. That deal is off the table. Pollard told my partner and I everything. Man, Pollard buggered you real good. Are you an anti-man? He said you picked the victims up with your minibus after they got through customs. Then you blew them away. One by one, then took their monies and valuables."

A spasm of irritation crossed Basdeo's face. He balled his cuffed hands into tight fists, his knuckles turning white. He gritted his teeth and rolled his eyes. A crazed look gripped his countenance as he snapped out his words with screams of exasperation.

"Joe Pollard can say what he wants! But how did I know those passengers were loaded with monies and valuables?

He, Pollard, working with an intake officer funneled me the information. That's how the operation went down."

"So Joseph Pollard was your finger man?"

"Call him what you want, Detective. He'll call me from my home and tell me when a flight from New York or Toronto is coming into Georgetown. The intake officer working the floor will identify the target passenger and tell Pollard, who in turn calls me."

"And you did the remainder of the job."

"Sure. I couldn't do it without the help of Pollard and his buddy."

"Where's all the booty?"

"How on earth will I know, Detective?"

"We'll meet at Pollard's house in Felicity and split the money and jewelry three ways."

"What's the name of the third man, the intake officer?"

"Glen Warner. He works at night on the screening floor. He lives in Providence Township."

"Want to thank you for being straight up, Mr. Basdeo," Brogan said.

"Look here, Detective. If Joseph Pollard is going to rat on me, I'll be damn if I don't do the same to him. All of us are going down. Not only me. I wouldn't take the rap for his ass."

"All three of you fellows are in more trouble than you all think."

"I don't care, Detective Brogan. Let them hang my ass. But I'm not walking to the gallows all by my lonesome."

"That's on you, Mr. Basdeo."

Martin Brogan and his partner exited the interrogation room. Simultaneously the two uniformed ranks went in the room and took Basdeo back to his holding cell.

"The chips are down now, Alan."

"You're sure right. At last you got that punk to tell it all."

"That's a result of good old police work."

"Old man Kilkenny might get a hard-on when he hears this."

"Sure, that old timer is going to Tiger Bay tonight to get laid."

The detectives walked along a long hallway. They were met by a sergeant in charge of internal affairs.

"Good work Brogan. I looked at everything via a monitor in the adjoining office," the man said as his face brightened with a broad smile.

"That's your job, Sergeant Weaver. Is it not?"

"Sure. I'm just saying that you were adroit in getting a suspect to confess to murders he had no intention of talking about."

"Thank you, Sergeant. Please make sure you get the report on the Captain's desk as soon as possible and another to the prosecutor."

"Right away Brogan."

Less than twenty four hours later, warrants were issued by a Georgetown magistrate for the arrest of Joseph Pollard and Glen Warner. A task force of detectives and uniformed ranks gathered at 2:00 a.m. at Timehri police station on Madewini Road about two miles from Cheddi Jagan International Airport.

"You ranks were briefed in detail about this operation," the leader of the task force told his men in a conference room. "Both individuals we are about to apprehend will be booked as accessories to murder in the first degree. The felonies were willful, deliberate and premeditated. Any questions?"

A silence hovered in the room as the lieutenant continued.

"Four ranks will go to the intake area of the airline. We know our target. A thin, pot-bellied man in his forties with navy blue uniform. His name's Glen Warner. Detective Ramsammy will issue the warrant while the ranks make the arrest. Simultaneously, five ranks will go to Joseph Pollard's office and execute an arrest while Detective Brogan issue the warrant. Anyone has anything to add."

No one spoke.

"OK, men," the lieutenant blurted, "let's get ready to put some bad fellows out of commission."

By 2:30 a.m., a convoy of police cars moved quietly along Madewini Road. At 2:45 a.m., the lawmen got out of the vehicles and filed out into the airport. Bystanders and airport workers were stunned when a group of uniformed ranks merged towards the British West Indian terminal area. Quickly an intake officer named Glen Warner was arrested, handcuffed and hauled out of the building without a struggle.

At the same time, five uniformed ranks and a detective made their way to the supervisor's office on the upper floor. They bustled through the door. A man named Joseph

Pollard was seated at a desk drinking coffee. Instinctively, the uniformed ranks surrounded him.

"What in hell you gigolos want?" Pollard barked.

"You're under arrest, Mr. Pollard. Let's see your hands!" all the ranks shouted.

"You buggers better have a warrant!"

"I've got a warrant here, Pollard. Accessory to murder," Martin Brogan said sharply.

"You riffraffs got to be crazy!" Pollard said pushing his desk forward and backing to the wall. And at the same time swung his right hand at Brogan. "Nobody is arresting me! That's not happening!"

The blow knocked Brogan backwards as it caught him plum on the jaw. Black streaks blurred his vision as he saw ranks piling on Pollard. The man was shouting as panic dominated his wild vicious face.

"I didn't kill nobody!" Pollard panted as he hammered a blow to a rank's midsection.

"Put your hands behind your back, mister," one rank cried, as Pollard hit the floor on his knees.

"This son-of-a-bitch is strong," another cop roared as their quarry broke loose his left hand and hit him hard over the cheekbone.

After a few minutes, Joseph Pollard was lying on the floor, hog tied, chest heaving laboriously like a wounded walrus.

"Let's go, Pollard. Get on your feet!" the unit leader shouted as three ranks struggled to get him off the floor.

Quickly the prisoner was hauled down the stairs and stuffed in a squad car as exasperated onlookers gazed with puzzled faces.

Later at Timehri police station, Pollard was asked to make a statement.

"I'm not saying a fart till I see my attorney."

"It's your right, Mr. Pollard," Detective Brogan answered.

Joseph Pollard's charges were upgraded to battery on police officers and resisting arrest. Quickly, he and his co-conspirator, Glen Warner, were transported to a Georgetown jail.

Chapter 26

Later that morning the detectives stopped for coffee at a Robb Street diner.

"Heard you had a fight on your hand, Martin."

"Say that again. That piece of garbage thought he could resist arrest and fight with the police. But we worked him over good."

"Any bumps or bruises on you?"

"Got caught with a punch on the jaw during the scuffle. It's a little achy. But as per regulations, I've got to stop at the hospital to get a medical report."

"Martin, it was tactful the way you got each fella to rat on the other."

"It wasn't ethical. But in this job you'll learn that criminals don't go by any rules. Sometimes as a detective, one has to get devious and conniving just to elicit a confession."

"That's why three bad guys are behind bars."

"And the evidence against them is strong and unshakeable."

"So what's next?"

"Tomorrow Kilkenny will brief us on our next assignment."

"That's the nature of the job."

"How are you and Julie doing, Alan? You ironed out your difference, I guess?"

"In a way. We agreed to tie the knot sometime next year."

"You mean that, Alan?"

"Sure. I love Julie."

"Detective Ramsammy, I'm happy for you."

"Thanks, Martin," the other man said as a triumphant grin shot across his face. "See you tomorrow at police headquarters."

"That will work."

The detectives left the diner and got into their separate cars. Brogan cranked the Toyota Corolla and hung a left on Camp Street and a quick right on New Market. After a few red light stops, the route was straight to the Georgetown Medical Center.

He displayed his badge to the triage nurse, taking the temperature of an old man.

"Be with you in a minute, Detective," the young woman said.

"Take your time. No rush."

Ten minutes later, the nurse directed Brogan to a cubicle area. He sat in a chair next to an examination table. She took his information on a sheet.

"What's the problem today, Detective?"

"Just here for an evaluation. I was punched on the left jaw while making an arrest."

"Sorry to hear that, Detective. Show me where you got punched."

"Here," Brogan said pointing to his left jaw.

The nurse donned a pair of latex gloves and touched the area a couple of times.

"Does that hurt?"

"A little."

The nurse recorded Brogan's vital signs and told him a physician was going to see him.

Thirty minutes later, a man in his early forties, dressed in a lab coat with a stethoscope around his neck, appeared in the cubicle. In his hand was the sheet compiled by the nurse on a clipboard.

"Good morning, Detective Brogan," the man said in a deep Cuban accent. "I'm Doctor Arturo Montoya."

"Nice meeting you, Doc."

The man took a pair of latex gloves from his lab coat pocket and put them on.

"Are you in pain?"

"A little."

"Open and close your mouth."

Brogan complied.

"Does it hurt when you do that?"

"Not much."

"OK. Your jaw is not fractured. It's a contusion or bruise. I'll give you a prescription for pain. You should be all right in a week."

"Sounds good to me."

The doctor whipped out a prescription pad, scribbled some writing on it and gave it to Brogan. "That's Motrin. I hope you feel better."

Brogan left the hospital with a copy of his treatment form and headed to his home in Cummings Lodge. Nadira was in the kitchen washing dishes when he got there.

"Martin," she smiled jauntily. "I missed you last night."

"I missed you too, Nadira," he responded as his face flushed with happiness.

"You were gone for so long."

"Well, it's all behind us now."

"What do you mean, Martin?"

"Nearly a year after your husband was murdered, we were finally able to solve his case. Those involved are now in jail."

"Now I feel quietly satisfied. No evil goes unpaid, because I know the penalty will be severe."

"What's sad is that Cyril isn't coming back."

"I lost him, Martin, but I gained you."

He looked at her candidly as he felt an avalanche of joy cascading over him. She drew closer to him. Her buxom body tucked tight and her funnel shaped breasts lusty. He gazed into her Nordic face and discovered her eyes. Living fountains of the most magnificently dark, shadowy and deepening twilight, he had ever espied. They embraced and kissed. Her lips gentle and moist rubbing against his. Then his hands slithered about her body like a hungry pair of serpents. They found her fingers and gripped them. Bone, muscles and tendon, fragile things.

She made something like a sigh. "Martin," she whispered, "Martin. Please don't leave me."

He was gratified.

THE END

ABOUT THE AUTHOR

Mr. Seales is a retired Registered Professional Nurse. He worked in hospitals, prisons and psychiatric institutions for many years. He holds an Associate Degree in Applied Science in Nursing, a Bachelor of Arts in English Literature and a Master of Arts in Creative Writing. "Death Rode A Minibus" is his seventh book. Mr. Seales lives with his wife, Claudette, in an Atlanta suburb.